Raleigh's Page

RALEIGH'S PAGE

By ALAN ARMSTRONG

Illustrated by TIM JESSELL

RANDOM HOUSE 🏠 NEW YORK

For Brandon

Text copyright © 2007 by Alan Armstrong. Illustrations copyright © 2007 by Tim Jessell. All rights reserved. Published in the United States by Random House Children's Books, a division of Random House, Inc., New York.

RANDOM HOUSE and colophon are registered trademarks of Random House, Inc.

www.randomhouse.com/kids

Educators and librarians, for a variety of teaching tools, visit us at
www.randomhouse.com/teachers

Library of Congress Cataloging-in-Publication Data
Armstrong, Alan W.
Raleigh's page / by Alan Armstrong ; illustrated by Tim Jessell. — 1st ed.
p.   cm.
SUMMARY: In the late 16th century, eleven-year-old Andrew leaves school in England and must prove himself as a page to Sir Walter Raleigh before embarking for Virginia, where he helps to establish relations with the Indians.
ISBN: 978-0-375-83319-9 (trade)
ISBN: 978-0-375-93319-6 (lib. bdg.)
1. Raleigh, Walter, Sir, 1552?–1618—Juvenile fiction. [1. Raleigh, Walter, Sir, 1552?–1618—Fiction. 2. Adventure and adventurers—Fiction. 3. Indians of North America—Fiction. 4. Virginia—History—16th century—Fiction. 5. Great Britain—History—Elizabeth, 1558–1603—Fiction.] I. Jessell, Tim, ill. II. Title.
PZ7.A73352Ral 2007   [Fic]—dc22   2006008434

Printed in the United States of America   10 9 8 7 6 5 4 3 2 1   First Edition

We have too few knight adventurers. Who would not sell away competent certainties to purchase, with any danger, excellent uncertainties?

—Ben Jonson and John Marston, *Eastward Ho!, 1583*

CONTENTS

I

WINDING THE SPRING

Stillwell Farm, Devon
8 April, 1584

Mr. Raleigh—

As you've heard, Andrew will be twelve next birthday. He is strong, healthy, tall for his age, steady. He has good teeth. He can read and speak English, Latin, and French. He knows numbers and writes a fair hand. He finishes school this spring.

If you accept him for service, according to custom you will feed him at your own table and furnish him with the habiliments of a gentleman. He will be trained to ride, fight, hawk, and conduct himself according to the fashion. On his sixteenth birthday you will make him a gift of £4 in gold and the clothing, books, instruments, and items of daily use then in his possession.

I will deliver him to Durham House this month end.

Regards from your friend,
John Saintleger

Andrew was eleven, tall for his age, hair like wheat stubble, hazel eyes, big front teeth he'd not yet grown into. His smile was eager and unafraid. He was wiry from farmwork and managing horses. Helping his father build and repair around the farm, he'd learned carpentry. He liked the tools his father had taught him to use, their shapes and edges, what he could do with them. He and one of his brothers had built a tree house together, a fort they'd slept in sometimes and in which they'd stood off neighbor boys' attacks with acorns and rotten fruit. Andrew had thought he might end up a carpenter.

Then came the night his father asked him to hold up clearing the table after dinner.

"You and I are going up to London together as soon as you finish school," he said, raising his eyebrows and beginning a smile. "Listen"—and he read aloud his letter.

Until that moment, Andrew had no idea of his father's plan. His heart raced as he listened. An introduction to Walter Raleigh was the most valuable gift his father could give his son. Raleigh was a star at court! Andrew's teacher, Master Tremayne, said Mr. Raleigh was for America, exploring, finding gold, and settling English people in the New World!

Standing before his map day after day, arms waving, dark hair flying, his voice urgent, Teacher Tremayne had wound the New World spring in his boys, calling on them to name rivers, winds, sea-lanes, and islands. He'd drilled them so often they could draw that map in their sleep. Their nickname for him was "Maps." He was only a few years older, sent down from Cambridge without graduating because of some prank.

Andrew and the others had sat quivering like a pack of eager dogs panting to go for the game their master hunted as Tremayne jabbed his map. A fine spray of his spit caught in the sunlight as he exclaimed, "There, boys! There sits America, waiting for you!"

Tremayne held out his open hands as if making a gift. "At college we read Richard Eden's *Travels,*" he said. "He called the New World Eden: gold, pearls, deep soils, trees taller than steeples and almost as large around, men's coats made of yellow and blue feathers, healing plants, furs, crops of corn they get with little effort.

"And this, boys!" he whispered. "No landlords fattening on us with their rents, rules, and leases; no sheriffs snatching up fees and fines; no church you must attend, no priest to pay!"

"He could get in trouble if Mr. High Sheriff heard him talk like that," Andrew's desk mate whispered.

"Aye," he replied, "but in America there's no High Sheriff. It's all free and open!"

"And there's gold!" his neighbor said with a nudge. "That's what I'd go for!"

Andrew's family name was Saintleger. "Salinger" is how they say it in Devon. He was the youngest, so he'd inherit nothing: the farm with its leases and debts would go to his oldest brother. His father could have put him to anything. His middle brother had been sent to clerk for a childless soap-maker at Bristol—future enough for him, but Andrew's father knew this son wanted a chance to make his fortune in the New World.

On the last day of school the students stood in line to say goodbye to their teacher. When it came Andrew's turn, Master Tremayne put both hands on the boy's shoulders. Andrew's jaw trembled. He loved this man.

"You're off to London to be page to Walter Raleigh!"

"If he keeps me," Andrew whispered, his eyes wide.

"Do your best and he will! No matter what, don't give up!"

Tremayne paused and shook Andrew in a friendly way. "Bring me news."

"I will, sir, I promise!" the boy replied, nodding, his face glowing.

2

THE ROAD TO LONDON

At home the night before he left, Andrew stayed up alone in the kitchen. It was like an old coat, warm and fragrant with the last of supper's roasting apples. He packed and unpacked his saddlebags, sorting things to take and things to leave.

He went upstairs to the cold attic he shared with his brother. He was after his box of birds' skulls, rare stones, feathers, and a button of stamped bronze his father said was Roman. Back down by what was left of the fire, he unwrapped each thing, weighing it for taking. With a long sigh he put them all back; what would they have to do with his new life?

He fell asleep with his head on the saddlebags. So his mother found him when she came to start the fire. She didn't scold. His father was already out seeing to their horses. Andrew couldn't eat that morning. He was too excited.

His mother and sister, Jane, his brother Paul, and all the farmworkers, even Nan, the old woman who'd helped when he was a baby, had gathered on Stillwell Farm's spooned-out steps to cheer the travelers off.

"Don't come back talking like a Londoner!" Jane called with a laugh.

"Or wearing silk pants," Paul added.

There was joking and teasing as the farm dogs milled and rowled about, yipping and barking. People stumbled over them, waving and yelling, "Hurrah, and good luck!"

"Come, boy!" his father called.

The horses started moving on their own. Andrew's heart was full to splitting, like an apple in the fire. "Goodbye!" he called so loud his voice squeaked. He blinked back tears.

He was glad but scared setting out. Having to leave home was no surprise. He'd known when he started school he'd be off to make his own way when he finished. He'd been trained to leaving like a soldier. Even so, his breath caught. A soldier, if he survives, can go back home and take up life again; for Andrew there would be no going back, except to visit.

"A fine morning we have, son!" his father said.

"Yes, sir," was all Andrew could manage right then. His head was full of the people he'd left on Stillwell's steps.

Where the track to the Saintleger farm crossed the way to the next, a sturdy black-haired girl stood with a small bouquet wrapped in cloth. Her skin was West Country dark, her lips bright. Her hair was tied back with a raveling string of red yarn. Andrew gasped when he saw her.

"Good luck!" Rebecca said as the boy slowed his horse. Her face was shining as she handed up the parcel. As Andrew took her gift she wiped her eyes, waved, and ran toward home. His throat was tight.

"Goodbye, and thanks!" he croaked.

"It's hard for them, being Catholic and so open about it," Andrew's father muttered as they rode on. There were rumors the girl's father had sheltered a priest. Under the new law he could be jailed for that. Andrew's father had been questioned and told to keep a watch. He'd said nothing. He was not one for that sort of business.

Andrew stuffed the flowers in his jacket. A string of beads was wound around the stems, a Catholic's rosary. There would be trouble if he was caught with it—a token of the outlawed religion.

He rode silent as his face cooled. The horses worked around sloughs, ruts, and holes that could trip an animal if taken too fast.

Birds sang in the soft air. The grass was thick and tufting under budding trees like pale-colored mists in the clear spring light. Yellow flowers opened like tiny suns along the ditches; in shady places bluebells massed like low clouds. Every place has its own fragrance. No matter where he'd just been, if you dropped Andrew blindfolded in Devon in early spring, with one breath he'd know he was home.

Suddenly he thought about where he was going and the man he hoped to serve. His heart jumped. Teacher Tremayne had said Walter Raleigh was all for settling Englishmen in America, but he'd never heard Mr. Raleigh spoken of at home, and now he was off to meet him!

"Tell me about him, sir," Andrew blurted. His voice was strong again.

His father, startled, half-turned in his saddle.

"Mr. Raleigh," the boy explained.

"Ah! Well, I hear he wears his fortune on his back," his father laughed. "And by story going around he'll toss it at the Queen's feet, which leads men at Court to credit him with more than he has."

"What story is that?" Andrew asked.

"They say he was walking with the Queen at a damp place after a shower. He was wearing a silk jacket embroidered with pearls. Seeing how the path was, he stripped it off and laid it out for Her Majesty's step. The loss of the jacket was nothing compared to the favor he gained with her and the swelling of his reputation at Court. The jacket cost more than he earned in a year, but the credit he gained in the Queen's eyes was worth that many times over."

His father paused. "Generosity can trick the cautious out of their caution," he added slowly. "Not that Mr. Raleigh intended, but he's capable of tricks."

"Do you trust him?"

"By report, the Queen does," his father answered, "and she's a good judge. Anyway, I wouldn't be taking you to him if I didn't think he'd be careful of you."

The two were riding side by side now.

"How is it you know him well enough to be taking me to him?" Andrew asked.

For a long time his father didn't answer. Andrew looked over at him, wondering if he'd heard.

"The story stops with you," his father said finally. "One January when we were boys, it got so cold the river at home froze over shore to shore. Our families forbade our going on it, but we did. Always the bravest, Mr. Raleigh went out ahead. I could feel it heaving, then the ice cracked under him with a boom like a cannon shot. He dropped straight in and it closed over. For what seemed forever I couldn't find him. Then there was his face, awful-looking, and I broke him free and dragged him to shore. I've still got scars from the ice cuts," his father said, holding up his arm. "I got him to a neighbor's. They gave him spirits. We never talked about it and you must not."

At noon they ate what Andrew's mother had packed in their saddlebags. At dusk they stopped at The Swan, drawn as much by the smell of roasting meat as by the bold sign hung out over the highway— a great white bird with orange bill and feet and bright gilded letters underneath.

There were fragrant herbs strewn with straw on the floors to take manure and mud. The Swan offered every kind of country food and sleeping mats of straw in the large room upstairs.

The boy had dismounted and was turning away, glad to be stretching and standing, when his father called sharply, "Andrew! Grab up your saddlebags!"

He pointed to an enclosure by the pump, where they stripped and waited for a boy to bring a square of soap and crisp rags to dry with. The pump water was so cold it made Andrew shrink.

As he started to open a saddlebag to get fresh

clothes, his father shook his head. "No, son! Wear what you rode in and keep your purse tied close to your body, even in bed. And your saddlebags—keep them beside you. What you would keep, keep tight. As for our clothes, you know the old verse: 'He that is small need fear no fall.' Act small."

Andrew's father was usually careful about his clothes. Now he pulled back on the splattered hose he'd worn. He didn't even flick off the clots of mire and dung on his boots. His jacket was smeared. He didn't brush it.

As he finished dressing, he turned and said quietly, "Keep to yourself about where you're from and where you're going." The way he said it gave the boy goose bumps.

"Is my going there a secret?"

"Mr. Raleigh has enemies and there are spies," his father replied. "The Spaniards and some at Court fear his plans for America."

Andrew shivered. "Who are his enemies? What are his plans?"

"To dinner, boy! I'm starved!"

They had plenty to eat—the meat they'd smelled roasting, fresh bread, vegetable stew, new lettuce, green beans in butter, custards, cakes, dark ale. Though clean to burning at the skin, in their dirty clothes they looked and smelled like plain ignorant folk. So they were taken. They sat at the common table, but no one sat close and no one asked them any questions.

Bed was a lumpy pad of straw wrapped in coarse cloth. Sharp ends stuck through. Andrew and his father lay down together in their clothes, heads on their saddlebags, purses tied tight to their bellies.

The boy took long shuddering breaths as he lay picturing his farewell at Stillwell and Rebecca's face as she'd handed up the flowers. He dozed off picturing Mr. Raleigh throwing down his coat. Then a mouse scritching after the crumbs in his saddlebag and the half-heard noises from the others who'd come up to sleep and snore in that room inspired his dream of Spanish spies sneaking after a shadowy coatless figure.

3

ENCLOSURE MEN

"What does Mr. Raleigh look like?" Andrew asked the next morning as they set out.

"I don't know," his father answered. "I haven't seen him since we were boys. Beyond his looks, though, it's his mind that draws the Queen. 'One man with a head on his shoulders is worth a dozen without,' she says."

"Has he friends?" the boy asked.

"Many claim him; he claims few. He stands alone, watchful. He and the Queen have that in common. 'See everything, say nothing' is her motto. It could be his."

"Does he have a lot of enemies?"

"Ha!" his father cried. "More than friends. Those who envy his closeness with the Queen and what she's given him wait to pluck his feathers. He won't grow fat and sleep in silk; he'll die lean with everything risked."

Andrew opened his eyes wide. "Mr. Raleigh? I thought he was rich."

"He wants glory more than fortune," his father said. "To win it he'll settle for a soldier's ration. 'Hope for England' is what Mr. Raleigh lives for."

A thrill shot through Andrew. Tremayne had talked about "Hope for England." That was America!

For a while they didn't talk, lulled by the noise and rhythm of riding, the damp sweetness of the new morning, the horses' comforting smells. Sheep dotted the velvet fields like clouds drifting across a green sky.

"When Mr. Raleigh was a boy," Andrew's father said suddenly, "his situation was like yours, only harder, because no one at home had a friend at Court to send him to. There was nothing to stay for, so he went to the wars, first in France, then Ireland. He took what courage offered and learned to swallow fear. He'll test you. He fought his way to London; you're riding in on a hired horse. He weighs such things."

"How will he test me?" Andrew asked.

His father shrugged. "I don't know. He has ways."

Andrew clenched the reins. He didn't like tests.

His father guessed what he was thinking. "There's a story going around," he said, "that soon after the

Queen first noticed Mr. Raleigh, they met in a gallery of the palace. As he knelt before her, he pointed to what he'd just scratched on a pane of glass: 'Fain would I climb, yet fear I to fall.'

"She took the diamond he'd written with and wrote below, 'If thy heart fail thee, climb not at all.' As she turned away, she pocketed the jewel."

His father twisted around in his saddle and smiled. "You'll climb, all right! You have a strong heart!"

That made Andrew warm inside. His father wasn't one to praise.

The road was yellow clay, sticking and heavy after the night's rain. It was rough underfoot, overhung with trees and brush. It was drowsily quiet save for the steady noise of the horses' walking and the creaking of their saddles. No wind stirred. The sky was blue and cloudless.

Suddenly Andrew's mount shied and nearly tossed him as two men leapt without a sound from the brush on his father's side, one waving a heavy stick, the older one an ax. As the ax man swung, Andrew's father's horse reared, neighing and flailing its hoofs. The swing went wild; the ax man staggered and fell.

At that moment, a boy jumped from the ditch on Andrew's side, thwacking at him with a club as he grabbed for the saddlebags. A blow landed hard on Andrew's knee.

His horse jumped and kicked. The strap the scrawny boy was tugging at loosened and tangled his arm. He screeched as his head slammed like a bell clapper against the pitching saddle. It was all Andrew could do to hang on.

Then the strap broke and the boy fell free. He and Andrew caught eyes. His were wide with pain, his

mouth an "O" of fear. He scrabbled into the brush like an injured animal as Andrew's father drew close, yelling, "Go! Go!"

A mile on in an open place, they slowed the sweating horses. Andrew was pale.

"Who were they?" he asked between clenched teeth. His knee was throbbing.

"Enclosure men," his father muttered as he dismounted. His face was tight. "Too weak and poorly armed to be regular robbers. Did he hit you?"

"My knee," the boy said.

"Can you move it?"

Andrew tried not to wince as he lifted his foot from the stirrup. It hurt, but he wanted to be brave for his father.

"Can you ride?"

"Yes."

Concentrating on riding took his mind off the pain.

They rode side by side, silent until Andrew asked, "What are enclosure men?"

"Folk forced by landlords off their fields and out of their cottages so the land can be enclosed for sheep," his father growled. His face was dark. "Necessity makes men dangerous," he added as if he were talking to himself.

Where they stopped that evening, the large cheerful mistress of the place noticed the boy's limp.

"What's the matter, lad?" she asked kindly.

He shrugged. "Nothing, ma'am. I fell."

As they sat at supper, she came by with a small jar and tucked it beside him. "Balm for bruises and sore joints," she said quietly. "I make it myself. Use what you need."

The men at the long table talked loud, but the boy hardly heard as he gorged on fat mutton, chicken, and heavy bread to fill an emptiness that wasn't hunger.

He went up to bed in the attic dormitory. He smeared some of the woman's balm on his leg. It burned. It had a strong odor. As he lay sleepless in the dank room, he saw the dragged boy again, his mouth twisted in terror. A chill went over him, but at last he slept, dreamless.

The balm helped. By morning his knee was better. As they left, his father handed the woman her jar with a coin.

"No," she laughed, pushing away the money. "I've got a boy. Boys is always off to tricks and getting hurt like that."

4

MR. RALEIGH'S COLLEGE OF THE NEW WORLD

"Durham House will be your college," Andrew's father announced as they set out on their last morning together. "With Mr. Raleigh and his people you'll learn mathematics and geography, even some of the new medicine. If you're lucky, you'll get your wish to travel."

It was early afternoon when they approached the London wall. Andrew smelled the ditch outside before he saw it—a dump for rubbish and dead dogs. Going through the gate, they passed into a noisy warren of close-packed houses built out over narrow twisting lanes. They approached a square where there was a crowd. At its center a slight figure floated in a space apart, white and sparkling in an apple green gown. She had red hair.

"The Queen!" Andrew's father called. "Touching folks for the King's Evil."

"What's that?" the boy asked.

"Scrofula it's called, an awful hardening and lumping in the neck that pains and scars. It's thought to be cured by the touch of royalty."

Suddenly a great cheer went up: "God save Your Majesty! God save Your Majesty!" As she turned and waved, the crowd stilled.

"God bless you all, my good people!" she said. Her voice carried like music.

The people cheered again as she returned to her work, touching the scarred ones.

Andrew was amazed that one so fine would touch those filthy people. He watched as the Queen caressed their sores boldly, seeming to grow more splendid as she moved through the crowd, her parsons chanting their prayers as loud as they could. A steward walked behind, giving each of the touched ones a small gold coin—the coin they called an angel.

"Is her touch a cure?" Andrew asked when his father drew close.

"Faith makes it so," he said. "Whatever the cure, believing in it makes it more powerful."

Andrew wondered what Mr. Raleigh would make

of that. From what he'd heard, faith and believing counted for little to the man he was going to serve. To Mr. Raleigh, cold proof was all.

They rode on slowly, struggling to stay together as they dodged rushing people, lurching carts, cows and sheep being driven to slaughter, clerks and children dashing on errands. Smokes and smells came in waves, at one moment bread baking, then stenches of tanneries, fat renderings, waste, garbage. The din was like the crash of wind and water in a thunderstorm. Bells rang. The boy had never heard so many clanging and clattering together. He held tight to the saddle; he felt dizzy.

They stabled their horses. As they stepped out from the stable's darkness into the bright street, Andrew's father whispered, "Beware of pickpockets." The boy's scalp prickled.

Durham House was plain compared to others on the Strand. Behind the white columns out front it was dark gray stone with towers, battlements, and turrets.

A sturdy, broad-bearded man in livery admitted them, "WR" embroidered large in red silk on his jacket. His beard was well brushed, the color of steel, wide as a spade and pointed like one. He wore a blade at his belt.

"I am John Saintleger," Andrew's father said. "I'm here with my son Andrew to see Mr. Raleigh."

"Yes, sir," the man replied, nodding so deep his whiskers touched his chest. "You are expected." He looked at Andrew and winked. "Welcome, lad." The boy tried to smile, but his mouth was tight.

The grim outside of Durham House misled. Andrew caught his breath as they walked in. He'd never been in such a grand place! Gleaming furniture was set about on floors of polished oak with Turkey rugs. The windows were large, some set with colored panes like church windows. The walls were oiled walnut panels with mirrors and rich tapestries. Patterns were worked in white plaster in the ceilings. It smelled of spice and lavender.

They were led across a large hall, up a broad carpeted staircase, then to a far corner and a spiral of stone stairs.

At the top there was a landing and an oval door of thick oak planks with heavy iron fittings.

Their guide knocked.

"Yes!" came a voice, not deep.

"James, sir," the man bellowed. "Come with those as you said was coming."

"Yes!"

James pushed open the door and stood back.

Andrew's father went in first. Mr. Raleigh leapt up, arms out in greeting.

He cocked his head when he saw Andrew. "I was

expecting a boy," he said with a smile. "You've brought a lad. More better." He had a small voice and the broad accent of Devon.

Andrew studied him as he spoke with his father. He was tall and quick, with dark skin and curling brown hair. His face was long, the forehead high. His beard turned up at the point. His eyes were small and heavy-lidded. He had a fighter's nose, scarred, wide, and flat. The fit of his jacket and hose revealed the toughness of the man within. His shoes were of soft felt, black.

His smell was sweet, a scent like hyacinth. It seemed to come from the man himself. Tremayne had said Alexander the Great smelled sweet: it was in his sweat, he'd said, a clue to his influence over men. Knowingly or not, everyone responded to it. People of evil odor made Andrew wary, not for their power but for their weakness.

"So, now, Andrew," said Mr. Raleigh, taking up the letter Andrew's father had sent proposing the boy for service. "'He can read and speak English, Latin, and French. He knows numbers and writes a fair hand,'" he read aloud.

As Andrew caught his breath and glanced at his father, Mr. Raleigh tossed the paper aside and addressed the boy in French.

Andrew answered. Again Mr. Raleigh spoke to him in that language. Again the boy replied in his slow, sure way.

"Bien," said Mr. Raleigh, narrowing his eyes and picking up a sheet with a column of numbers. "Add them," he ordered.

Still standing, Andrew did so. He checked his work twice, then handed back the scrap.

Mr. Raleigh glanced at the sum. "Right!" he said with a grin. "Sit down." He cleared a space on the narrow plank that was his desk. "Let's see the 'fair hand' your father says you write."

Andrew wiped his face on his sleeve. He was sweating but his hands were freezing.

Mr. Raleigh gave him a page to copy, then turned to his father.

Andrew worked carefully but suddenly his quill snagged on a lump in the sheet. There was an ugly blot.

That's it, he figured. He sighed a shuddering breath and was about to quit when he remembered Tremayne's farewell: "No matter what, don't give up!"

So he finished. He wrote the last part clean and easy, free of all awkwardness.

He stood up when he was done. Mr. Raleigh was showing his father the model of a new ship he'd designed. The boy looked around. The room was like a ship cabin, everything compact, built-in. From the two narrow windows, Andrew saw sails colored white, tan, and red, mast tops, horses, carts, people on the wharves, the river coursing like a huge pulse.

Mr. Raleigh broke his marveling with a call and a sudden motion.

"Hi, Andrew! What's this?"

He tossed a rock studded with square yellow cubes that looked like metal.

"Gold?" Andrew stammered as he stumbled to catch it, his face flaming.

"Bah! Fool's gold!" Mr. Raleigh barked. "Pyrites brought to the Queen, worthless except as ballast. Better they freight with sassafras.

"Do you know sassafras?" he snapped as he glanced at the blotted sheet.

Andrew nodded, too scared to answer.

"Speak!"

"My teacher spoke of it, sir."

Mr. Raleigh handed the boy a withered root.

"Smell!"

He could already. It was unlike anything he'd ever smelled before.

"The drug sellers work it into pastes and tonics for the dread Spanish disease of the privy parts," Mr. Raleigh said in a mocking voice. "They give equal weight in silver for it. Because the leaf is shaped like the groin, by their doctrine of signatures it heals the ills of that place. Physicians' logic: if this leaf looks like a lung, it must heal afflictions of the lung. Do you believe that?" he asked.

Andrew stood dumb like a pig poisoned. It was what his mother's book said. She collected plants for medicines according to that principle.

"Have you no tongue?" Mr. Raleigh growled.

"I . . . If the physicians do, I believe it, sir," Andrew stammered.

"Yes!" said Mr. Raleigh grimly. "So they would have it. I'll teach you to question! Our doctors study ancient texts, but they don't look inside the body to figure how it works and the ways of illness. I do! Against the law, we dissect the dead. How else to learn the secrets of living?

"I know medicine," Mr. Raleigh continued as he paced. "I use leeches to let blood, maggots to eat corrupted flesh, rhubarb for stoppage of the bowel, honey and tar water for cough, lemons for scurvy. Those cures work by experience," he went on as he snatched down jars and vials from his shelves.

"I give you nothing for these, costly though they be—this one, say, a potion of ground pearl, or this of powdered mummy, or this," he said, handing Andrew a corked jar, "the most precious drug in my collection and the most worthless! Unicorn's horn. Perhaps if you believe in the beast you'll believe in the cure."

He was scowling, standing close.

"Some physicians advise their patients to suck emeralds. Better you suck soft eggs. Most doctors can only say whether you will die of what ails you; the cure is beyond them. What say you to that?"

Andrew stepped back, almost falling.

"I don't know, sir." The boy's face was hot. He looked to his father for help.

Mr. Raleigh nodded. His face was smooth again.

"You will once I've taught you," he said with a thin smile.

"You blush," he went on. "You may hide your thoughts but your color gives you away. Better you hide your feelings than your thoughts. Folks will remember your color long after they've forgotten what provoked it.

"Listen," he said, bending close, "make as to laugh when you feel shame. It will throw off your opponent and keep your blood down."

Raleigh turned to his desk and picked up what Andrew had written. "This will do," he said. "You got better as you went on. Try warming your hands before you write. Our scientific man here, Mr. Harriot, can't write anything one can read because his hands stay cold and stiff.

"Now! James!" he yelled. "The drink!"

The liveried man came in with cups of something Andrew had never smelled before.

"Cacao," Mr. Raleigh said. "*Chocolate* to the Spaniards. They learned from the Indians in New Spain to drink it for a tonic. I got this supply from one of their ships we captured, a prize just brought in. This drink is a fruit of piracy," he said with a smile.

A bitter one, the boy thought. The drink was mud brown. He drank what he could get down. Moments later his blood began to pound.

Raleigh had turned away to show Andrew's father his globe of the world. The book on his chair was open to the image of a plant. Andrew looked closely. It was not familiar. His mother had taught him plants.

Mr. Raleigh's eyes followed Andrew's. "Monardes's *Joyful News of the New Found World,*" he announced. "A Spaniard curious about medicine plants found in America. Are you interested in plants?"

"Yes, sir!" the boy said firmly. He had command of his voice again.

Mr. Raleigh smiled and nodded. "Then you will make a summary of that book for me and we'll see how your mind works. You like plants? Come!"

He led them to his gardens above the river. The tide was dropping fast. The water made a hushing noise like wind, flickering where the light caught it. It was dark and silty. There were things floating in it.

"My gardener is a Frenchman," Mr. Raleigh announced. "Do you know why he's here?"

"No, sir."

"Because he's a Protestant, one of those they call Huguenots. We persecute our Catholics, they persecute their Protestants—all under the sign of the cross. He was a tree-grafter for a nobleman before they smoked out his faith. He fled with his green knowledge and a clutch of cherry cuttings. Fortune comes in many coats. What that man knows about plants has made his.

"Monsieur Pena!" he called.

A square man with hair the color of iron appeared in rough clothes and a stained leather apron that fell below his knees. He was older than Andrew's father. His skin was olive tan.

"Sir," he said with a slight bow.

"Monsieur, this is Andrew and his father. Beginning tomorrow you'll be the boy's tutor," he said, seizing Andrew's right hand and holding it out palm up. "Tough enough, you see. No need to be gentle with him."

As the Frenchman nodded, he gave Andrew a smile that lifted the boy's heart.

Mr. Raleigh turned and pointed to rows of new shoots in a series of neatly groomed beds.

"Those plants were taken off the Spanish ship we captured with the cacao. The priest on board was carrying a leather case of seeds and roots. In the sea fight he went overboard. Monsieur Pena will raise his plants if anyone can, but I wish they'd spared that Jesuit. Judging from his things, he knew more than prayers.

"May be some good things for you there, John," Mr. Raleigh called to Andrew's father. "Anything promising we'll make sure you're the first in Devon to have!"

"Thank you, Walter!"

They walked to the orchard. The lightness of the Frenchman's step belied his bulk.

"Cold nights, the Monsieur wraps these trees in cloth like Egypt people wrap their dead," Mr. Raleigh laughed as he pointed. "In the dark they look like giant ghosts. Thanks to his tricks, I bring the Queen baskets of cherries before her gardeners do."

He paused. "Monsieur: please send my friend John home with slips of your best for him to try."

Andrew's father beamed.

As they were walking back past the well-ordered beds, Mr. Raleigh stopped suddenly and turned to the boy. "My neighbors grow roses. I experiment to find what will feed our explorers in America. You will help Monsieur Pena with this work."

Andrew looked hard at the plants. He'd write Tremayne about them: here was proof of Mr. Raleigh's plans!

When they got back up to the turret, Mr. Raleigh rang his bell.

A tall page appeared, "WR" embroidered on his jacket.

"Peter," he said, "welcome Andrew, on trial as the new page. He has a fancy for plants to match your fancy for music. Settle him and arrange his needs."

Andrew's father embraced his boy as they parted. "Do your best," he whispered. "For all of us!"

5

ANDREW'S NEW HOME

Andrew had a weakness that came on sometimes when he got scared. His strength would go out for a moment—like when you throw a fresh log on the fire and the flame gutters and almost goes out before it catches again stronger.

When he and Peter got into the hall, it hit him. He couldn't get his breath. His knees went weak. He sagged against the wall. He knew it would pass, but at the moment it was embarrassing.

"What's wrong?" Peter asked. "Homesick already?" His voice was cold. There was no reading his face.

"Something I ate," Andrew replied. "I'm all right."

Peter was broad-shouldered, with long blond hair. His face was smooth, unmarked. Andrew steadied himself. Panting slightly, he walked beside the older boy.

"You're from the West Country, like Mr. Raleigh," Peter said. His voice was deeper than Andrew's. "Will your father go with him to the Queen?"

"I don't think so," Andrew replied.

Peter studied the newcomer without talking as they went down the long hall. His eyes were slate.

He was graceful, no motion wasted, but his teeth were crooked. He was conscious of them and kept his mouth shut except to speak.

"Where are you from?" Andrew asked at last.

"Ireland. When my father comes to London, he goes to the Queen with Mr. Raleigh."

Peter said nothing more as he led the newcomer to the dormitory, a long, high-ceilinged white room laced with thick oak beams. Small-paned windows opened on the Strand. There were three beds, each with a gray, rope-handled seaman's chest at the foot. Three desks were lined up under the windows. There were no pictures or ornaments on the walls, just a wooden peg beside each bed. Two were hung with towels.

The third page came in. William was younger than Peter. He was stocky, with bristling black hair cut short. Measles had roughed his skin. He smiled and stumbled as he made to hug Andrew welcome. His feet were big and so were his hands. Andrew was taller but skinnier.

Peter made a sour face at William's greeting.

"Show Andrew the place of necessaries," he ordered. "I'll meet you back here after he's bathed."

William led the younger boy down the hall to a dark stone closet in a corner closest to the river. Andrew had to back in, crouching; it was barely wide enough for the holed seat. The shaft emptied into the river.

"It's no place to linger," William laughed as Andrew crept out, "and when the cold wind blows up off the river, you'll want to go before you've went."

They smiled together and walked close, talking fast as William led on to the bathing room, larger and cheerfuller, with windows high up. There were stone basins to pour water in, with a wooden plug for each, and a rack for buckets. William gave Andrew a towel, a heavy square of soap scented with lavender, and a boxwood comb. "This is for cleaning your teeth," he said, handing the newcomer a string of waxed silk and a pot of charcoal.

As Andrew bathed, William told him how he and Peter had come into Mr. Raleigh's service two years before.

"I'm thirteen, he's fourteen," he said. "We've

been presented to the Queen. Our tutors at Court are teaching us how to lead soldiers, dance, and manage hawks."

"Do you and Peter study with Monsieur Pena?" Andrew asked.

"No."

Andrew wondered if that was because they were richer. The other boys' fathers had estates and fine houses, but Peter and William were younger sons too and on their own as Andrew was. They had more behind them, though. They wore gold signets; Andrew had no ring.

They met Peter on their way back to the dormitory. He was no friendlier than before as he led them up to the wardrobe, a small sun-filled corner room on the floor above theirs. There was a mirror on one wall, shelves with mounds of folded cloth, canvas-covered forms like statues, and in the corner under the windows a workbench awash with scraps of every color and shape, bits of chalk, measuring tapes, scissors, and thread ends. A large figure was bent over the bench, humming loudly.

"Hello, Mistress Witkens! Hello! Hello!" William called as loud as he could. He kept his voice deep.

Slowly the figure straightened and pushed herself up from her bench.

"This is Andrew," William yelled as she turned slowly toward them. "Andrew! The new page."

A smiling pink face framed in a mass of straggling gray hair greeted the three boys. As she pushed her hair back, colored thread ends caught in her curls. She was quilled like a hedgehog in front, her black wool work apron stuck thick with threaded needles and basting pins.

"Ye catch me without me cap, lads!" she bellowed as she groped for what looked like a large white bag. "I pull it off to see better."

"He'll be needing suits like ours, Mistress," William hollered.

"Oh, he will! He will!" she sang in a deep voice as she pulled the white bag over her head and patted it into place. "And as soon as I fit him up, he'll pop out of 'em, which is the way it is with you boys!

"Hello, new boy!" she yelled. "Andrew, are you? You look promising, Andrew! Take off your jacket and stand up there," she said, gesturing to a low, rug-covered platform.

"Yes, madam," he said. Andrew liked her. She reminded him of a countrywoman he knew back home, his mother's best friend.

Humming like a hive of bees, Mistress Witkens

gathered up measuring tapes, strings, a sheet of paper, and a charcoal pencil and set to work.

As Andrew took off his belt, Peter pointed to the dagger he'd worn traveling. "Have you ever used it?" he asked.

"Only on a bag," Andrew replied.

"I've used mine on a man," Peter said with a grin that showed his scagged teeth. "In the street, as pay for one who made to pick my pocket. I killed him."

The way he said it sent a chill through Andrew. He knew Peter was swaggering, but it wasn't a lie.

Once Mistress Witkens had finished her measuring, the three boys went back down to their room. "Show him what's in his sea chest," Peter ordered as he flopped down on his bed to read.

William showed Andrew the silver spoon and blade he was to use at table. Wrapped in silk was a small dragon made of silver, its tail a toothpick, its head an ear spade. There were also quills, paper, a lead inkwell, and an ivory-handled penknife.

William chatted as he handed over those things. It was as if he were making gifts. For a moment Andrew forgot his strangeness. Then he remembered he was at Durham House, on trial. Perhaps what he was holding had been used by a boy who'd failed.

He stiffened and muttered, "Never!"

"What?" asked William.

The younger boy shook himself. "Are these things new, or were they used by others before?" he asked.

"A boy before," said William. "There was a test. He lied. Mr. Raleigh sent him off."

Andrew had lied sometimes. He wanted to know what that boy's test was, and his lie. Before he could

ask, Peter came over with his lute. The new page's coming had made an afternoon's holiday for them.

"Do you sing?" he asked Andrew.

The boy nodded. He had a fair voice. He knew songs. "And I have a flute," he said.

"Get it and play for us."

Andrew played "Oh Noble England" better than he ever had before. William smiled and nodded approval as he kept time. He went and got his fiddle. Soon the three pages were playing and singing rounds together. Andrew's voice was as high as Peter's was low. William's straggled in between. They did part-singing like Andrew had done in school. It felt good to sing. It sounded wonderful.

6

MR. HARRIOT

The man who lived in the set of rooms beyond the dormitory came out with his fiddle when he heard their music. William introduced Andrew. The man's hands were cold.

Mr. Harriot was tall and sallow, with black hair thinning at the front and a stark black beard that against his skin appeared almost blue. His eyes were black, large as almonds. He was a little older than Andrew's teacher back home.

He had an easy laugh and sang tenor. Until the bell for supper the four of them made music together. Then Mr. Harriot led them down to the dining hall.

"It will be a clear night," he told Andrew as he headed to his place. "The light lasts long now, so after supper I'll take you up to the roof and show you

London at dusk through my glass. I call it a perspective cylinder. When it gets dark I'll show you the stars!"

Tremayne had told his boys about glasses for looking at a distance, but Andrew had never seen one. "Thank you, sir," he said. "I'd like that."

Mr. Raleigh usually dined at Court. That evening, though, he ate at Durham House, seated at his high table. The rest of his household, forty in all, sat ranked below him.

Monsieur Pena and Mr. Harriot sat several places above the pages; Andrew sat below Peter and William. Mistress Witkens sat a few places below Andrew, her white bag cap perched and bobbing. James, the guard who'd admitted him that morning, sat next to her. He caught Andrew's eye and winked again.

They all watched Mr. Raleigh. No one was to begin eating until he did. He poured gravy on his gleaming silver plate, broke in bread to sop, then sprinkled on salt from an elaborate silver container shaped like a ship.

Andrew waited for Mr. Raleigh to lift his spoon. He didn't. Instead, he signaled the man standing behind him to carry his plate to the crone with wild hair, who sat at the last place.

The room was silent. She muttered a prayer in

Latin from the old religion. Mr. Raleigh then took his meal out of a wooden bowl like everyone else.

"Who is she?" Andrew whispered to William.

"A holy woman," he replied. "Sometimes she stands out front in the Strand chanting the old prayers. She tended the chapel when the Catholic bishop and his priests lived here. When the Queen ordered them out, she wouldn't leave. Mr. Raleigh said she could stay."

Andrew looked around the hall. The crone and Mistress Witkens were the only women; guards, servants, and soldiers made up the rest of the noisy company.

William nudged his new friend. "Did you notice what Mr. Raleigh took his salt from?" he whispered.

Andrew nodded, looking up at the silver ship again.

"The Queen gave it to him as a mark of favor," William said quietly with a proud smile.

Peter ate fast, saying nothing. When he finished, he interrupted William's whispers. "My father served with Mr. Raleigh in Ireland," he said, loud enough for everyone around to hear. "They both have large holdings there. The natives are rebellious. When I complete my service here, I'll go as officer with the army in Ireland. 'Blood and iron for the natives!' my father says. 'No conciliating!'"

He pressed his thin lips so tight together his mouth went white as he fixed his eyes on Andrew. "Do you know Ireland?" he asked.

"No," Andrew answered.

Peter turned away.

Other talk at their table that night was that Mr. Raleigh was just back from seeing two exploring captains off to America.

When Mr. Harriot finished his meal, he came and sat with the pages. "To the spies on the docks and in the taverns, the rumor is our expedition men are pirates out for prizes," he reported. "They'll keep what they catch, sure enough, to help pay for the voyage, but their main business is finding a base for our investigators."

Andrew's breath came short. Everything Tremayne had said about Mr. Raleigh's plans was true!

Mr. Harriot asked the new page friendly questions about his family and schooling. He wore plain black like a Puritan, but the boy soon learned he was not one of those.

"What do you do here?" Andrew asked.

"I tutor Mr. Raleigh in the new mathematics and

help his navigators with their maps for deep-water sailing. Maps lie flat," he explained, gesturing with his hands. "Mr. Mercator's new projection makes the shortest distance from England to America appear a straight line, but since the earth is round, the shortest way is really a curve. I show the mariners how to allow for the curve of the globe and correct the sea compass. Mostly, though, I study things about America to get ready for going."

Andrew bit his tongue to keep from saying that was the thing he dreamed of.

"And I am employed by Mr. Secretary Walsingham, the Queen's chief spy," Mr. Harriot continued, "composing and breaking codes."

"Are you a spy?" Andrew asked.

"Watch who you ask that of," Mr. Harriot laughed. "Some might think you rude. Anyway, as the saying goes, 'The Queen's eyes are in every place.' My eyes are in service to hers. Sooner or later yours will be too.

"Now!" he announced, standing up. "To the roof! In the last light I'll show you a bit of London." Andrew nodded, smiling and grateful but dizzied by so much new and strange.

When they got to the roof, Mr. Harriot reached into the pocket of his long black coat. "Here," he said, handing Andrew a brass tube. "Astronomy is what I like best. This is my device for looking at a distance."

Andrew put it to his eye. Suddenly he could make out deckhands on ships in the Pool, then, some distance down the Strand, a red-faced man telling another a story with big gestures and laughter the boy could see but not hear.

"I fashion these myself with lenses I have made from rounds of glass I get from the glassblowers," Mr. Harriot was saying. "I buy the ones with the fewest waves or bubbles and take them to a Jew in Amsterdam who cuts gems. No Jews here and it is our loss."

Andrew wanted to ask why there were no Jews in England, but Mr. Harriot was eager to go on about his lenses. "My friend in Amsterdam shapes the glass for me, working the rounds like a potter on a wheel, cutting with tools of crystal and polishing with garnet paste. I calculate the curve he must cut to from pictures in a book from Baghdad. What I'm learning now, my Arab author knew five hundred years ago."

"What do you mean, your 'Arab author'?" Andrew asked.

"The Arabs were great astronomers," Mr. Harriot replied. "They built on what the Greeks knew. I have an ancient Arab astronomy book I got from a Turk trader out of Constantinople."

"We saw Turks at Plymouth," Andrew said, eager to add something to the talk. "A Turk trading ship foundered on the rocks off Plymouth and put in there. Some of the crew had fever. The town doctor wouldn't go to them because he said they kill Christians. My mother went and tended them."

"What were they trading?" Mr. Harriot asked.

"Cloves and cotton. They paid her in spice and cloth."

"Good trade for us, if we could get it," Mr. Harriot mused.

As the sky began to go from pale gray to smoky purple, dots of light came on like someone lighting candles far away.

"There's the waning moon. No planets now, but stars," Mr. Harriot explained. "That one over there is the North Star; to the left, higher, the Big Dipper," he said, helping Andrew aim.

Through the brass cylinder Andrew saw stars closer than the eye ever brought them, but he was more eager for Mr. Harriot's talk about America. He wished Tremayne were there to hear it.

Before Andrew could get Mr. Harriot away from his stars and back to the New World, Peter and William came up to join them for a quick game of catch in the last light.

They used one of Mr. Raleigh's tennis balls. Mr. Harriot said they were stuffed with the hair of poor women. It was a point of honor that no ball go off the roof. The last time his turn came, Peter threw hard over Andrew's head. As the newcomer leapt to catch it, he nearly went off the roof himself.

Mr. Harriot scowled as the shadow of a smile flickered across Peter's face. Andrew felt sick. *Already I have an enemy,* he thought.

7

THE BOY WHO FAILED

That night, Andrew lay awake in the strange bed. There were noises from the street. William's bed was next to his. Peter was asleep in the bed beyond William's.

"Are you awake?" William whispered.

"Yes."

"Are you going to Court tomorrow?"

"I don't know. First thing, I go to school, to Monsieur Pena."

"Oh," murmured William. "I was going to show you my hawk."

"The boy who was sent away," Andrew asked, "what was his lie?"

William turned and leaned on his elbow. Andrew could just make out his face.

"Charles's family was rich. His father was dead and his older brother, who'd inherited everything, was sickly. He said he wished his brother would hurry up and die so he'd inherit and be page to nobody.

"Mr. Raleigh had a leaky vessel on the river. Charles was sent to measure the water in her. Mr. Raleigh told him it would take some doing—shifting cargo to lift a center plank, then mucking around in the ballast to measure to the hull.

"Charles was from the Midlands. He was used to ordering farm laborers about; he didn't know sailors. They're proud and independent, each one responsible for the whole ship. No landsman puts on airs to them—even if his father does own a thousand acres! Well, Charles goes out to the ship and tells the sailors to do his task. They wouldn't. They said the bilge was filthy and the last man who'd touched it got plague and died horrible. They gave Charles a candle and warned him to go careful with it—the bilge gas might catch fire and blow him up.

"The next morning, Mr. Raleigh called us to the turret and had Charles tell us his test. We were never to tell anyone what Mr. Raleigh put us to: he's a great one for secrets!

"So there we are, lined up like soldiers, and he has Charles step forward.

"'What was the depth of water in the bilge?' he asks.

"Charles says so-and-so much.

"'Did you measure?' Mr. Raleigh asks.

"Charles nods.

"'Speak!' says Mr. Raleigh, so loud we all jump.

"'Yes.'

"Then Mr. Raleigh pushes his face so close to Charles's he falls back into me.

"'Ships have been lost to such a lie,' Mr. Raleigh whispers. He's one of the Queen's admirals, you know. There's nothing about ships he doesn't know, so he wasn't playacting. His face was black!

"He tells Charles that on top of being a liar he was too proud to ask for help and a proud liar is a threat to all. 'Go!' he yelled. He yelled it so loud Charles jerked like he'd been hit! It made us all jump. And so he sent him off."

Andrew's face was as hot as Charles's must have been.

"How did Mr. Raleigh know?" he gasped.

"The sailors came and told him."

Andrew didn't sleep well that night. He dreamed about the boy who'd been sent away.

He was never homesick when he boarded at Tremayne's school. Now a hot ball of feeling rode high in his chest.

8

ANDREW'S FIRST DAY AT DURHAM HOUSE

The bells at dawn awakened him before the others. For a moment he imagined the morning starting at Stillwell Farm; then he gritted his teeth to keep from thinking about what he missed. He got up and bathed and made his way to where they'd eaten dinner. No one was around. He heard voices at the front door, where James, the doorman who'd greeted him yesterday, stood outside in the Strand making notes as tradesmen came in—bakers with fragrant hot loaves, a carter with milk, another with vegetables. A giant of a man staggered under the butchered half of a cow across his back.

"You hungry, boy?" James called in a friendly voice when he saw him. Andrew nodded. "Then come with me and let's see what the cooks can do for us. I'm hungry too!"

He pulled the door, bolted it, and led Andrew down to the kitchens. Already there were good cooking smells and much activity. James got them mugs of hot milk and hunks of the new brown bread. He dipped his bread—"To ease my teeth," he said, making a face. "Going out on me fast!"

Later, at regular breakfast, Mr. Harriot came and sat beside Andrew. There was no order to the seating at breakfast, but no one sat at Mr. Raleigh's high table. Monsieur Pena joined them.

"By your leave, Monsieur," Mr. Harriot said, "I have an hour's bit of business at Court this morning. May I take Andrew with me to give him a quick look and then return him to you?"

The Frenchman nodded. "You show him the flowers at Court, then I'll show him what we grow here. Be off soon, though—it looks like rain, and Court colors run."

Andrew half-trotted to keep up with Mr. Harriot's long strides as they walked the Strand from Durham House to Whitehall Palace. They held to the center of the street to stay clear of the slops—and worse—folks tossed from upper windows. They dodged carts, women hawking cockles and oysters from baskets around their necks, the salt man making deliveries from the box strapped to his back.

"What's your business there?" Andrew panted.

"Solving a small problem in mathematics for the upcoming lottery," Mr. Harriot replied. "The government expects to sell thousands of tickets across the nation. For the last one, they sold four hundred thousand, but there were problems sharing out the returns. The counting went slow, and some complained they never got their due. I've worked up a better counter— a sheet of cloth the pay agents can lay on the counting table to work out the divisions by shuffling tokens. Mr. Raleigh put me to it."

The road they walked ran right through White-hall, a village unto itself, where palace men swarmed like gaudy butterflies in silks and gloves and feathered hats, for all the morning was warm. They seemed to walk small as they made large gestures and wagged their heads. Andrew didn't see any women about.

"Is today special?" he asked. "This is grander than Lord Mayor's Day back home at Plymouth."

"No," muttered Mr. Harriot as they turned down a corridor. "Just an ordinary Monday in spring with the gallants out flaunting."

"What is their work?" Andrew asked.

"Showing off to each other and begging favors from the Queen," Mr. Harriot laughed. "They own land. Their tenants keep them in finery."

They entered a room marked "Lottery Office." Andrew watched close as Mr. Harriot talked numbers and shuffled the pieces, explaining to the officer how the new counting cloth and tokens would make division easy. The man's eyes glazed over.

"So, clear enough?" Mr. Harriot asked at last.

The lottery officer scrunched up his mouth and nodded weakly.

"Good. You'll demonstrate it to the lord commissioners and send word to Mr. Raleigh. He waits to hear.

"They'll have me back," Mr. Harriot laughed as they walked out. "That poor fellow can't count beyond his fingers—like most of them," he said, gesturing at the fops around. "They look down on tradesmen and merchants who soil their hands with money, but if you handle money or try following a mapped course, you learn how to count quick enough."

Hurrying back to Durham House, they passed the great yard where men in armor trained for combat on horses, spearing and dodging bright-colored tethered balls the size of a man's head. Andrew thought he recognized Peter. He waved; the other didn't.

The bells hadn't struck ten when he joined Pena in the garden. The Frenchman was mixing something in his wheelbarrow.

"You've heard about men who mix strange things

together to make gold, yes? Well, we gardeners do alchemy too," he said, pointing. "In this bin we have ground limestone; in that one, wood ash; there, seaweed. The others are washed sea sand, peat, oak leaf mulch, cow dung well rotted. In the farthest ones, the stinks—fish meal and chicken droppings. We work to make the right soils for the Spanish seedlings.

"I've divided the plants among a dozen plots: one sweet with lime, ash, peat, and fish meal; one sour with oak mulch and dung; some sections sandy, some loose with seaweed. The farthest one is simple London clay and river muck. Your first job every morning will be to mark the progress of each plot. Once we see where the seedlings thrive and where they fail, we'll move them around.

"Then to the work every gardener knows: on your knees for the battle against weeds! Always we have weeds. They come like Spanish spies in the night, hiding until they make themselves secure and deeprooted, and then they rise and prove tough to pull. So now I show you what is weed and what is worthy. It is easier with plants than with people, and there is this difference: if you pull up something you want to keep, you can always replant it. With a dead man, no."

He handed the boy a triangle blade on a pole.

"You loosen around . . ."

Andrew showed what he knew. He'd weeded in his father's beds since he could walk. It was the same thing when Pena demonstrated how to prune: Andrew knew the art.

Every few feet there were shallow dishes, some with small gray bodies floating. "Slugs," Pena explained. "We trap them with beer. The other pests we pick and pinch. As for crows—stone them!"

When the noon bells rang, Pena led Andrew to a large shed filled with pots and tools. "Here we put away," he said. "We wipe the blades clean and sharpen what we've dulled. They are precious, these edge tools—French, the best." Andrew felt a pang: the shed's smell reminded him of the one at home, and Pena's words about caring for the tools—they were like what Andrew's father always said when they finished work together.

Dinner was served when the bells struck one. All the Durham House folk took their places for the main meal of the day: slices of roast beef, as much as anyone could eat, dark bread, and warm ale. Many then went off to sleep.

Although drowsy himself from the heavy food, Andrew slogged up to Mr. Raleigh's turret and began work writing a summary of the Spaniard's book of American plants. Knowing what he did of his master's interest in drugs, he concentrated on those plants with medicinal properties. In the best hand he could manage he began an extract of what Señor Monardes wrote about tobacco: "A medicine leaf chewed or smoked that strengthens the heart as it stirs up the blood. . . ."

His head was heavy. The air was still. He put the pen aside and laid his head on his arm. Suddenly he heard Mr. Raleigh on the stairs. As he struggled to look alert at his work, Mr. Raleigh's eyes took him in. Andrew was sure the man knew he'd been sleeping. Mr. Raleigh nodded and said nothing.

9
HOMESICK!

His third night at Durham House, Andrew called out in his sleep. Peter heard. "The baby cries and whimpers 'Mamma' in the dark," he taunted as they dressed the next morning. "Perhaps Mamma's precious should go home."

Andrew clenched his teeth and made fists as he struggled not to cry and not to fight. His father had warned him against brawling.

"You called out other names too," William told him later, when they were alone. "Nothing I could make out before I shook you quiet."

Pena guessed something was wrong when Andrew came to work. "It is hard at the beginning," the Frenchman said, looking into the boy's eyes and nodding slowly.

Andrew bit his lip as Pena put a sweaty arm around him. "Courage!" he said. "I know. I had to leave home too.

"But look here!" said Pena, pointing to a new plot he'd staked out. "You will make this your own garden," he said, picking up his tools. The knot in Andrew's chest loosened.

Pena sang a silly verse he made up as they worked the ground together:

I'm a man of the dirt,
Which does no man hurt,
As it feeds him and clothes him
And saves him from Sin.
The pretty ones hurry to wash it away,
But without it they wouldn't be here today.
They think it low to dig and delve,
But it was dirt that fed the Twelve.
Hey!
Hey!

Andrew began to smile as Pena sang loud, clowning and pretending to plow:

Adam's delving, so they say,
Helped him work his Sin away;

We do the same, every day,
So we have no Sin to pay.
Hey!
Hey!

As he finished with an elaborate bow, sweeping his leather apron to one side, Andrew grinned and clapped. He felt better than he had in days.

"Ma foi!" Pena exclaimed. "They are too serious here. With them it is all work and no laughing, with this for the Court and that for the fortune. Even their play is work. This evening I take you into the streets for play! We'll be safe together."

"I'd like that!" Andrew cried. "I've been once to Court but never to town."

"Good!" said Pena, beaming. Then he looked hard at the boy. "Your color is bad. Are you well in your gut?"

Andrew looked down and shook his head.

"Ah!" the man exclaimed. "Your guts grip because you eat no salads as they do in France. Come! I keep a bed for greens! Every morning now when you come to me you will eat leaves from my patch. All that meat, all that bread," he said. "No Frenchman from the South, no Florentine, not even a Spanish peasant suffers in the gut like you English. And do you know why? Because you do not eat fresh leaves like the other animals."

He made Andrew eat a fistful of salad leaves. Some were bitter.

After supper Andrew walked close beside Pena as they joined the slow tide of people out for pleasure—gaudy-dressed women, groups of sailors laughing and talking in their own tongues, country lads like Andrew looking around with new eyes. They drifted past musicians playing for a coin, acrobats in orange-and-green costumes, mimes with chalked faces. A hushed crowd watched a man pick his way over an alley on a rope stretched high. Every time the ropewalker teetered, Andrew felt the bottom go out of his stomach. He hated heights and tight dark places. The man twisted and danced and swayed for what seemed a long time before he slid down to get their money in his hat, a red felt cone with a ring of large orange spots at the crown.

"Who is he?" Andrew asked.

"A Turk," Pena said. "The Queen allows them the run of the city because they fight the Spanish. 'When in danger from one country, play the other against it' is her policy."

The next moment, they passed a man reciting a ballad he was selling about the recent capture and torture of a priest named Campion. Andrew drew close to hear—Rebecca had spoken of this priest. At the top of the paper there was a smeared picture of the man's last agony. The boy's stomach lurched as his knees went weak.

"Ha'penny, lad," the hawker called, handing over a copy. "See the dead Jesuit!"

"No!" Pena exclaimed, pulling Andrew away. "You've no business with any of that."

At the corner a fruitier and his stout wife offered dark red cherries in twists of scrap paper. "Kentish cherries, my lovely!" the jolly lady called to Andrew as she flourished a cone. "Take one of my cherries, darling! First of the season, here and nowhere else! Sweet, sweet, my sweet!"

Pena bought a twist. They walked silent together, chewing and spitting pits. "Sweet they are, but not as good as what I sent the Queen ten days ago!" Pena laughed, wiping his chin. Andrew was amazed. They were huge compared to the cherries they grew at Stillwell.

As they approached Durham House in the dark, a whoosh of fire erupted from a barge on the river as a rocket sizzled up, flaming silver. Andrew threw his arms over his head.

"No fear! It's just Mr. Harriot at his tricks," Pena cried. "He practices to amuse the Queen. Fireworks are her favorite toys. That man uses gunpowder the way cooks use flour," he continued as they got to the door. "He gave Mr. Raleigh a snake to surprise her. When she touched its tail with a spark, it spat fire from the front. She jumped. She ordered a dozen more to scare the ambassadors."

Just then Mr. Harriot came running up, holding his hands. They were blistering red and his cheek was smudged. "You saw my fire show?" he cried, trying to smile. "I got singed. One of my rockets," he said, grimacing.

"Cold water! Cold water!" Pena yelled as James opened the door. "Andrew—bring leaves from the Spanish plant we study this morning."

Andrew hurried down to the garden. It was hard to see in the dark. He felt among the plants in the special bed for the fleshy spike-leaved one Pena called aloe. He tried breaking off a leaf. It bent but wouldn't break, so he stripped off his jacket, dug carefully, and carried up the whole plant.

Mr. Harriot spoke between his teeth as Pena smeared jelly-like sap on his hurts.

"Tomorrow night," Mr. Harriot panted, "the Queen progresses downriver sitting in the glass box atop her royal barge. She wants a show with drums and trumpets for people on the riverbank. Mr. Raleigh will give her that and more: ten floats like the one we just tested, spaced out along her route. A hundred rockets . . ."

"And if one of those singes her," Pena laughed, "you'll send for Andrew and his Spanish remedy, yes?"

10

ANOTHER TEST

Andrew had been at Durham House a week when he
was summoned from the garden. Mr. Raleigh told him
to go to a geographer he knew to borrow a map.

"Take in the man," Mr. Raleigh said. "Doctor Dee
draws maps according to his angels."

The boy's eyes widened. "He draws according to
angels?"

"Yes," said Mr. Raleigh, nodding. "He will tell you
he speaks with angels through his magic glass—a ball
of smoky crystal made in the Orient long ago.

"Men come upon strangeness traveling in
dreams," he continued. "Doctor Dee is a dream traveler."

*Angels? Dream travelers? Is the man joking with
me?* Andrew wondered.

Mr. Raleigh's face was serious as he went on. "A

remarkable thing about his maps is what he leaves off. Most maps show the rumored islands of the ancients. The doctor strips away to what is known.

"Yesterday," Mr. Raleigh continued, "one of the Queen's agents came to me with a new map taken at Lisbon. There was a strange island marked in waters I know well.

"'What's this?' I asked the spy.

"He told me he'd asked the same of the man who'd drawn it.

"The drawer told him it was called Wife's Island because, while he drew the map, his wife sitting by asked him to put in a dot of land for her so that she, in imagination, might have an island of her own."

Mr. Raleigh paused to study Andrew's face. Andrew's eyes were fixed on his.

"I need to see the doctor's new map," Mr. Raleigh said, narrowing his eyes. "No Wife's Island on it, I think."

He leaned close.

"In our work we must be able to persuade others to do our will even if it is not theirs. If you ask him right, he may lend it.

"They have told you about the page you replaced?"

"Yes, sir."

"You understand there are ways of asking?"

Andrew nodded.

"Good. The doctor is the Queen's fortune-teller. She pays him little to keep him hungry. She reckons a fat astrologer would sleep; she wants her man gnawed by hunger as he tracks her future.

"He knows medicines and poisons," Mr. Raleigh went on as he paced the turret. "He's given me things that kill in an instant, things that kill in a week, rings with points to carry venom, tainted salts and balms, a liquid to induce stupor. Above all, he's our best mapmaker.

"I want to see his new chart, but he's a quarrelsome man. If I asked he would put me off, saying he needed time to make it more perfect. I need it now.

"You will go first thing tomorrow in your country clothes."

Andrew was to tell no one who had sent him. If stopped for any reason, he was to swallow the message he carried, a bit of paper smaller than his hand sealed with a clot of red wax. The boy gagged at the thought of eating it.

Mr. Raleigh instructed him carefully: "Catch your boat at London Bridge and return there," he said. "Do not use my gate. The river men study everything. For a while at least I'd like to keep them unsure of our connection."

He gave Andrew a fourpence coin, a groat.

"Twopence up, twopence down, with tips in the bargain, so don't let the first charge you more or the second complain."

The next morning, a ferryman rowed Andrew up the river to Mortlake, where the doctor lived. From the boy's halting answers, the ferryman took him for a bumpkin seeking a relation.

Riding on water made Andrew queasy. He was sorry he'd eaten breakfast. He'd heard from William it was the same with Mr. Raleigh: to save his stomach he'd go down to London Bridge to cross the river rather than go by water.

At the Mortlake landing, he handed the ferryman his coin. The ferryman pocketed it.

"My change, please, sir," Andrew said.

"Change? Fourpence is the fare, boy."

"No, sir. Twopence is the fare from London Bridge, and that includes my thank-you."

A man had come up behind. "My change, please, sir," Andrew said again loudly so the man behind him could hear. "I gave you a groat. The fare from London Bridge is twopence, including my thank-you. The change due me is twopence."

With a grumble the ferryman gave him his change.

Although the day was cool, Andrew was in a sweat as he walked to the doctor's.

He'd expected to meet a stooped and musty old onion-eating scholar with gravy on his shirt and tallow in his beard. The man he met was tall and slender in a long blue velvet robe and black skullcap. He had a tapering white beard and shining dark eyes. His face was bright.

As the boy handed him Mr. Raleigh's note, the doctor gave him a halfpenny for his pains. If this was what Mr. Raleigh called quarrelsome, Andrew liked his quarrel.

The doctor came and stood so close the boy could feel his heat. His breath was sweet. He stared into Andrew's eyes. His look went deep. The boy struggled not to step back, blink, or look away. His eyes began to tear.

"How old are you?" the doctor asked at last.

"Eleven years, sir."

"Your eyes are older. You have taking-in eyes."

Doctor Dee studied Mr. Raleigh's note. "I am to give you a lesson in the new geography. Are you interested in that?"

"Yes! I'd like that!"

The doctor led Andrew into his study. He worked and slept in a large room crammed with apparatus, skulls, globes, books, and papers, separate from his family so no moment would be lost if one of his angels came to him suddenly. At any moment, he could begin where he'd left off. The north-facing wall had large windows to catch the best light.

As he showed Andrew his collection of instruments and ancient maps, he talked about exploring, measuring distances at sea, the mathematics of surveying and making charts.

The boy followed as best he could, but it was too much. The long showing and explaining left him drowsy. He was struggling to keep from yawning when the doctor said, "And this is my newest chart," as he unrolled the map Mr. Raleigh wanted.

Suddenly Andrew was all awake. The doctor's map was different from any map he had ever seen:

coastlines changed according to the latest surveys, fabled islands gone, new things marked.

"Only what we know for sure," the doctor said. "Only what the sea captains confirm."

Andrew wanted to ask for it, but something checked him; it was not yet the moment.

"Will you take dinner with me?" the doctor asked.

"Thank you. Please," Andrew answered. He was tense but hungry too.

The doctor rang his bell. A few moments later he pushed aside maps and instruments to clear places as his man brought pork pies steaming fresh from the oven, mugs of dark ale, and fragrant quarters of Spanish oranges.

As they began to eat, the doctor asked, "What is your plan of life?"

The friendly way the man asked made Andrew relax a little. "I want to go to America," he replied.

The doctor studied his face. "Yes," he said. "I saw that in your eyes. You see over the water. You have strong ambition.

"What will you do there?"

"Make a farm and trade, sir."

The doctor nodded. "My father was a merchant. A merchant must be nimble as a flea to keep fed.

"And later, if you become rich, will you come back to England?"

"I'm for America. I'll make my place there."

"Oh, but when you're rich you can buy a place here," the doctor said.

"I want to make my own, sir. A place for Catholics too."

The doctor looked up sharply.

Andrew blushed. He'd said too much.

The doctor nodded as he looked away.

"I understand," he said. "A few years ago the Queen gave her charter to a man who planned to establish a Catholic colony in America at Newfoundland. 'Put them away but keep them loyal' was what he proposed.

"He got swallowed up by the sea. Mr. Raleigh has his charter now. The man who drowned was his half brother.

"I helped him," the doctor said softly. "I drew his maps."

For a while they ate in silence. Then the doctor asked, "Does your horoscope show you becoming a planter?"

"I don't know."

"Has anyone cast it?"

"My father had a woman do it when I was born.

He wanted to know if I would live. Each of the three before me died before he could get named in church."

"Do you know your date and time of birth?"

"Yes."

"Then we'll see what you're to be."

He studied the marks in Andrew's fingernails and the lines in his hands. Then he brought out a large bronze disk he called an astrolabe.

"With this," he said, "I can figure the position of the planets and the stars at any moment of the year. Navigators use it to locate their positions east and west at sea."

The thing was heavy, with a hoop for hanging at the top. It bore strange markings. At the center there was a silver bar on a pin. He hung it on a hook over his desk, set the needle, and got out his zodiac book.

"What do the marks mean?" Andrew asked.

"This was made in Baghdad a long time ago," the doctor said. "The characters are Arabic numbers, degree marks, and names of the heavenly bodies."

Andrew thought about Mr. Harriot's brass tube for looking at a distance: here was the second instrument he'd seen since coming to London that had something of the Arab about it.

The doctor then brought out what he called his

magic eye, the crystal ball Mr. Raleigh had mentioned. He pored over it for a long time.

"I see travel and trading," he said at last. "You will get an honest sufficiency but not more."

He looked up. "More than sufficiency brings greater grief than less. Keep your conscience clean, and your teeth. Teeth are the guardians to health. Riches cannot buy a clean conscience or good health."

He unhooked the disk and put his glass away. Andrew wanted to know more about his future, but the doctor was on to something else.

"What have you noticed about Mr. Raleigh?" he asked.

"Nothing—I mean, everything, sir! I mean, I have just begun his service," Andrew stammered.

"Yes," said the doctor gently, "but what have you found most remarkable?"

Andrew stood bewildered. "What he knows about maps and plants, medicines, ships . . ."

The doctor was shaking his head.

"His scent?" Andrew asked at last.

"Yes, that," the doctor said. "It is sweet, yet he wears no perfume. What else?"

Andrew shook his head.

"He is like the kept dog in the Aesop fable," the doctor replied at last. "Do you know that story?"

"No, sir."

"One winter day at dusk a wolf came into a farmer's yard, drawn by the scent of roasting meat. The wolf was gaunt and ragged. As he approached the door, he was greeted by the farmer's dog. The dog was sleek. There was no getting past him, so the wolf stopped and bowed politely.

"'You are handsome, my friend,' said the wolf. 'How is it you feed so well?'

"The dog swelled his chest. 'I guard the farmer against robbers. For this he gives me all the food I want and a house by his door.'

"'Ah,' said the wolf. 'Do you think I might join you in this work?'

"'You have good teeth and claws to fight with,'" the dog said, studying the wolf. "'Perhaps he could use you.'

"Just then a flea annoyed the dog. He shook his ruff. There was a rattle of chain.

"'What's that around your neck?' the wolf asked.

"'The collar I wear to stay in place,' the dog replied.

"'Oh,' said the wolf. 'Then I think I'll be off. I'd rather be hungry and free than fed and not.'

"You see," the doctor continued, "the Queen feeds and houses Mr. Raleigh, but his leash is too short for him to sail to America. If his exploring captains give a good report and the expedition goes, he won't be along. The Queen keeps him tied to Court."

"Why?" Andrew asked.

"She cannot risk his loss. He is one of the few she can tell her mind to."

Doctor Dee grew silent. He looked at Andrew and nodded.

"You have a good plan. Your sign is friendly to adventure. Merchants are heirs to adventure, but your fortune will hang on winds—a fair breeze may bring your fortune, a storm sink it. Men will live better for your risks; your failures will cost them nothing. That's the way it is with merchants. London gets more intelligence from her traders than from all her scholars."

He paused.

"Avoid the trade in human flesh. Mr. Raleigh's sea dog friends Francis Drake and his kinsman John Hawkins do well by slaves, but it is an evil business. What one handles one becomes."

It was now late afternoon. The doctor had given Andrew dinner and the lesson Mr. Raleigh had requested, and he'd told the boy his future. It was time to leave, but Andrew didn't have the map.

He took a deep breath.

"Sir, your new map . . ."

"Yes?"

"It's like nothing we have," Andrew whispered.

The doctor looked at him steadily, saying nothing.

"We need it."

"He sent you for it?"

"Yes."

Doctor Dee nodded. He said nothing as he rolled up the map, tied it, and wrote a note to Mr. Raleigh. He didn't seal his note.

"Be careful when you make your copy," he said. "I have no other. Return it tomorrow."

"I will, sir. Thank you."

The doctor smiled as he reached out and hugged the boy goodbye.

On the boat downriver, Andrew opened the note:

"For the boy's sake I lend it. He will go. You will not."

11

THE CONJUROR

That evening, Andrew stayed up with Mr. Harriot through two rounds of candles, copying the doctor's map. The stink of candle smoke left him queasy.

"This is excellent," Mr. Harriot muttered as they worked. "The doctor has a nose for mariners' secrets like a fox's for rabbits."

Mr. Harriot kept rubbing his hands together. He noticed Andrew watching.

"They're always cold," he said. "Winter and summer, whatever I do. I sleep in mittens."

The next morning, Andrew ate nothing. He wrapped the map tight and took the ferry back up to Mortlake.

There was a strange hush about the doctor's place. His garden was trampled. As Andrew turned in at the gate, he saw books and papers strewn in the yard. The door hung on a hinge.

He called out.

No one answered.

The boy's heart began to pound.

Finally the doctor's serving man appeared in the doorway, ghastly pale, his eyes bright and darting like a cornered rat's.

"He's gone," he whispered. "People came in the night."

"People?" Andrew asked. He felt a chill.

"They called him a conjuror. 'He casts spells to make us sick,' they screamed, 'our animals too!'"

Andrew looked around.

"Who? Was it his neighbors?"

"I couldn't see," the man blubbered. "It was a mob. I ran to the cellar and hid."

"Where is he?"

"I don't know. He ran off in the dark when he heard them coming."

Andrew kept the map. As he left, he spied something black in the brush by the broken gate. It was the doctor's skullcap. He put it in his pocket.

Back at Durham House, he and Mr. Harriot took the map to Mr. Raleigh.

"He'd been warned," Mr. Raleigh said, fingering

the black cap. "We'd heard that Spanish agents were stirring up his neighbors. That's why I sent you when I did."

"Where is he?" Andrew asked.

"Safe," Mr. Raleigh replied as he turned and put the skullcap in the drawer beneath his writing board.

Andrew started to leave.

"Wait!" Mr. Raleigh called as he turned back. "Be careful what you write home. Use this ink our friend the doctor prepared," he said, reaching for a stoppered jug.

"We call it onion juice. It isn't, but that's what it smells like. Once the liquid dries, your writing will be invisible until the letter is gently rinsed with the doctor's tincture and held before a flame. Do you understand?"

"Yes, sir," the boy replied, "but how will I get the tincture to my family so they can read what I send?"

"Leave that to me," Mr. Raleigh replied, opening his eyes wide.

12

WILLIAM

Peter always fell asleep first. The two younger boys got in the habit of whispering back and forth in the dark, glad to have a friend to share things with.

One moonlit night they snuck out of the dormitory and crept downstairs. No one was up. They began a game of silent hide-and-seek, faster and faster, choking back cries and giggles as they swerved around chairs and hid behind and under, until William slipped on a rug and crashed into a table. A huge china jug went over. That brought James. He caught sight of Andrew's back as the boys scurried upstairs.

A cat got blamed for the jug. For days William's arm was so sore he couldn't hold his hawk.

A few nights later, Andrew couldn't sleep for being hungry. The boys glided down to the cellar kitchen. Andrew stirred up the fire to look around.

Again their noise brought James. They slipped into the larder as he came in. They'd left the bread box open. Next morning James told the cook she had a clever mouse, perhaps a pair. "Too small for rats, I'd say," he told her, raising his great eyebrows and pretending to peer around the door.

"You let them mice of yours know I'll be leaving for them under a plate," she chuckled. "No need they should gnaw stale bread!"

Thereafter she left out second suppers for the boys—plate-scrapings and remainders of the best things served at Mr. Raleigh's high table.

They had less and less to do with Peter. William would walk with him to Whitehall Palace in the morning for their hawking and jousting lessons, but all his free time now he spent with Andrew.

One afternoon Andrew took William to see the new shoots in the garden plot Pena had given him.

"Spanish seeds and roots," he explained. "We don't know what they are, so Pena says when they're grown, we'll have to try eating them—leaves, roots, fruits, everything—to see if they're food. He says we'll have to be careful, because some may be medicines to loosen the bowel or cure fever, and one root the Spaniards call potato, eaten green, can kill."

"Make a stew for Peter!" William whispered as

they made faces and put their hands to their throats as if they were gagging and throwing up.

"What are the bowls for?" William asked, pointing to the dishes set along the path.

"Flat beer to trap slugs," Andrew explained.

"Phew!" gasped William, looking close. "Serve that to Peter for his drink!"

William showed Andrew the heavy embroidered glove he wore for hawking and the delicate velvet hood worked with silver his bird wore.

"Do you want to hear how I whistle him back?"

Andrew nodded.

William scrunched up his mouth and blew a shrill piercing call that made Andrew wince.

"It's like his own," William said.

The glove was scored deep with claw marks.

There was a tiny leash with a clip that went on the bird's leg. "It's called a jess," he explained as he packed away his gear.

"Why do you do it?" Andrew asked. "Do you eat what it catches?"

"No," William laughed. "You think like a farmer—everything for food! It's for sport. It's something courtiers do, like dancing."

The two boys sang together and played duets, talked about home and their schools before and what they hoped to do when they finished Mr. Raleigh's service.

"Mr. Harriot told us before you came that you're for America," William said. "That's why Peter hates you. Mr. Raleigh is more for America than Ireland now. Peter's for Ireland. His father has the Queen's grant to thousands of acres there, but the Irish natives won't work it because they say it belongs to them. They kill the English he brings over. If he can't get tenants to settle and work his land, he'll lose it. Peter wants to go make those natives submit."

"What will you do?" Andrew asked.

"I'm training to lead soldiers."

"And later?"

William shrugged and rubbed his head. Mistress Witkens had just cut his hair. It was like rubbing a black bristle brush.

"What about you? What do you want to do?" William asked.

"Set up a trading station and make a plantation in America," Andrew answered.

"Out there? Away from everybody, like an exile? Why?"

"To make my fortune on my own land, free of landlords, sheriffs, and taxes!" Andrew exclaimed.

"Spoken like a farmer!" William laughed. "You'll

make your fortune, sure enough, but I'd miss London too much."

Andrew wanted to add the part about making a place safe for Catholics like Rebecca and her family, but he held back. His father had warned him to keep those things to himself.

William was good at drawing figures and faces. He'd snatch bits of cold charcoal from the fire to scratch a likeness of whomever he was looking at—Andrew, Peter, Mr. Raleigh, Pena, Mistress Witkens, James, Mr. Harriot. He got them all. Folks liked to be drawn. They'd pose until he'd finished, then they'd ask for their picture even though he'd scribbled it on a scrap of paper or some stiffened cloth he'd got from Mistress Witkens.

"How did you learn to do that?" Andrew asked.

"My mother taught me as she taught me to write my letters. I'll teach you."

Andrew's sketches were rough at first, but William made him practice. "Look and look again," he insisted. "Don't be afraid to smudge out what isn't right." For days he had Andrew draw circles and ovals to learn the shapes of heads and where ears, eyes, and mouths go. "For everyone it's the same," he said. "The sizes of heads differ, but where eyes are, the ears, the nose—that's the same."

Peter teased that the two of them would end up common face-painters.

"Let's make masks," Andrew suggested one afternoon. "We made masks for plays at my school—pictures we held on sticks in front of our faces for pantomimes. We did stories about the Romans and King Arthur and his Knights of the Round Table. Once we made masks of the big figures in town—the Lord Mayor, the High Sheriff, the Bishop—and paraded around for the other boys at school.

"We could do a play for Durham House—the fable of the fox and crow. Can you make the face of a fox and the figure of a crow?"

"Sure!" said William.

He drew a fierce crow with a bright black-dot eye on a board Andrew found by the river. Crow black was easy enough, but fox red? How to get that color?

Andrew went to Pena. Pena took him to the kitchen, where they got a pot and mixed pig's blood with flour and beet juice.

They rehearsed. Neither liked playing the fox, so they asked Peter if he would do it.

Peter wrinkled his nose and made sneering remarks about players and low-class street theater, but finally the chance to be the clever hero took him.

One night after supper, they gave their show in the refectory. Everyone agreed Peter made a good fox, sly and wheedling as he tricked the cheese from William the crow.

"What if you painted almost-likenesses of the Queen's head and Mr. Raleigh's?" Andrew asked that night as they whispered together.

"Why 'almost'? I can do them to the life," William protested.

"No. Make them just close enough to leave folks unsure."

William gave Mr. Raleigh a feathered hat and pointed beard. The Queen got a drooping nose under a flaming red wig. They hinged her chin so she could open her mouth.

Andrew held the Raleigh mask before his face and said Mr. Raleigh's lines as William pantomimed the Queen.

Mistress Witkens helped them with costumes, a length of fancy cloth for the Queen's gown, blue velvet pants and a yellow shirt for Raleigh. They made props. The cheese became a sack of gold and a long flapping title deed with ribbons. They also wrote lines for Mr. Raleigh's flattering.

"Madam, I hear it said at Court and even in the street that you are as kind as you are wise."

The Queen shuffled and swished her gown as she nodded, the sack of treasure and the deed bobbing in her jaws.

"Truly, madam, it is reported that your realm, rich and glorious as it is, is but a faint reflection of your beauty."

She tittered and bent her head in modesty as she fluttered her hands.

"And the lovely grace of your dancing, madam— it is the talk of every Court in the world and the envy of all women of quality."

The Queen jigged a little and did an awkward turn, nearly falling.

"But those envious women hiss to each other that your voice is sour and cracking. Surely, madam, your voice is a fair match to your radiant face?"

At that, the Queen opened her mouth to sing and dropped her treasures.

"Oh, madam, I am honored," said Raleigh, bowing low as he snatched them up, wrapping the title deed around his head like a crown and tucking the sack in his pants.

"Give it back!" the Queen yawped as she chased after Raleigh.

"Too late, madam," he called over his shoulder. "I'm off for America!"

They tried out their play for Pena in the garden shed. They could hardly act for snickering at their cleverness. Pena's grim face stifled their giggles.

"It is treason to mock the Queen," he said when they'd finished. "Men are locked away in the Tower for less. Worse, you insult the man who helps you. Your joke is like the taunts made behind his back at Court. Shame!"

Pena took the masks and broke them up.

"I do this as a favor," he said as he left with the pieces.

There was no whispering between the boys that night.

13

ANDREW'S LETTER HOME

Durham House
30 June, 1584

Dear Family and Rebecca,

    I am well. I miss you all, and the dogs. I haven't written before because I spend so much time writing for Mr. Raleigh, my hand cramps. My guts stopped up at first, but Pena, the gardener I study under, made me eat leaves and now I am better. He teaches me farming. We try Spanish seeds, but we have nothing ripe yet. Pena says this is because the English sun is not so hot as the sun in New Spain. He remembers Mr. Raleigh's promise that if we grow anything of profit we will send seeds to you for Stillwell. I have my own plot. One thing I grow

93

is a thick-leaved plant with sap that eases burns. Mr. Raleigh's scientific man burned himself with gunpowder, face and hands, and the sap of that plant healed him.

Pena puts frogs in the cistern and makes me watch them swim. He says he will teach me to swim in the river. I don't want to. The water is cold. Everything is in it. When the tide is out it smells. Nobody else swims here, but he does every day.

He laughs and makes up songs. He is never quiet. He works the soil with a hoe that has rings and bells on the handle. "Stink, stank, reek, rank/Rats along the riverbank," he sings as he digs. He sings as loud as he can. He took me for a walk along the river. We saw a Turk walking on a rope and a bear with a ring through its nose dancing on its hind feet as its keeper played a flute and beat a drum. These things are free, but some people toss pennies for them. Pena tossed a halfpenny in the Turk's hat.

My best friend here is William. We do plays together. He goes to Court for hawking and jousting. We made a play about people at Court, but Pena said it was mean. I don't like the tall page Father met named Peter. He acts highborn, but William says he isn't really better than we are.

I copy things for Mr. Raleigh until my hand hurts. He made me write extracts from his book about plants in New Spain. It says cacao and tobacco chewed together make the Indians so strong they can travel for days without food or water. Mr. Raleigh says he will make the experiment on himself. He takes no physician's word for anything!

He praised my extract of the Spaniard's book. When I told William at dinner, Peter yelled, "Good dog!" and made to pat me on the head. I barked and made him jump, so people laughed as much at him as me.

Sometimes I work with Mr. Harriot, studying how the natives live in America. Mr. Harriot will go there to write a report. He talks about America as much as Tremayne does.

Sundays, we go to services at St. Paul's Cathedral. Mr. Harriot took me down below, where sixteen men work the bellows that blow through four hundred bronze pipes. The smallest is the size of my hand. The tallest goes up to the roof. The low notes go so deep the floor shakes. The high ones sound like birds. Last week the Queen's preacher preached for two hours. A man goes up and down the aisles with a long black stick, poking those who doze off. He pokes a lot, men and women.

Yesterday William and I walked to the broad place in the river where ships dock. It is called the Pool. A sailor said some of the ships we saw were from India, Russia, and Constantinople. We passed the Tower. William says there is a deep pit there for the priests they catch. On London Bridge Tower the heads of traitors are stuck on pikes. There are dozens, like rotted squashes. I did not know we had so many traitors.

This halfpenny is for Rebecca for a hair ribbon. Mr. Raleigh's geographer friend gave it to me. He's called a dream traveler. I went to him to borrow a map. He saw my future in his magic glass, but I can't tell it, because Mr. Harriot said repeating it to anyone would be like pouring vinegar into milk: all the good will sour.

I think of every one of you every day and say my prayers.

Love,
Andrew

14

THE WINE MERCHANT'S CLERK

A few days after his visit to Doctor Dee, Andrew was again called from the garden to the turret. He met Mr. Harriot at the door as a small, shortsighted man slunk out.

Mr. Raleigh was pacing. He started speaking as they entered.

"Mr. Phelippes has just made report. He is one of Principal Secretary Walsingham's chief decoders. He's learned that a wine merchant in France has a new map showing the Spanish forts in the Caribbean. Our expedition will take on fresh water and provisions at one of the islands there. We need to know where the enemy is."

Mr. Raleigh turned to the window and spoke as if he were addressing the gulls that were always circling and calling.

"Mr. Secretary wonders if some of my people could get this map. We have little time before the merchant must return it to the official in Paris he borrowed it from.

"The merchant trades spirits for American furs," Mr. Raleigh went on. "He gathers information for the benefit of his trade and sells it to his Paris connection."

He narrowed his eyes as he turned back.

"Andrew, your father said you have a rare sense of smell. A wine dealer's chief instrument of trade is his nose. Do you have the nose of a wine dealer?"

"I don't know, sir."

"We will find out."

He pointed to a row of filled glasses, each one on a numbered paper, and an empty bowl.

"Sniff and taste. Match like with like. Swallow none: sniff and taste, then spit into the bowl."

Another test! Andrew thought, his heart pounding. He did his best as he sniffed and sipped from the first glass, spat, then sampled the others the same way to find its match. Most were sour to his taste, but the third matched the first, and so it went. It wasn't hard with the first three pairs. Of the seven glasses remaining, four were sweeter than the others. They stalled him.

His face was long as he set them aside and worked

over the other three. He made one pair. The stray was not like any of the others. He was angry with himself, afraid he'd missed something. The men were waiting, watching. He finally gave up and said he thought the sweets were all the same.

Mr. Raleigh's eyes were hooded. He took a paper and checked the numbers.

He showed it to Mr. Harriot. Andrew couldn't

read the man's face. Then Mr. Harriot grinned and said quietly, "You have the gift."

Andrew took a big breath as Mr. Raleigh resumed his pacing.

"So now we have a way of proving to the Frenchman that Andrew and his master are in the wine trade.

"Suppose," he continued after a moment, "that a wine merchant and his clerk were to call on the Frenchman, offering to trade wine for furs on terms advantageous to the Frenchman. And suppose further that one of the samples they offered had been touched with drug. The Frenchman might enjoy a nap while the boy and his master made a survey of his papers and took what they needed.

"There won't be time to copy."

Mr. Raleigh explained that with one of Doctor Dee's recipes, he'd made a tincture from the sap of poppies.

"The drug is tasteless, almost the color of water. A small drop in his glass will send a large man sleeping. It is called opium."

He turned to Mr. Harriot.

"Andrew will do for our clerk, but who will be our wine merchant? We need a plain-mannered stranger we can trust who speaks French."

"Me!" exclaimed Mr. Harriot.

"No," said Mr. Raleigh, shaking his head slowly. "Our connection is too well known. I need someone rougher in manner than you, someone the foreign agents have never seen here."

Andrew thought of Tremayne. He was rougher than Mr. Harriot, he spoke French, and he was no part of Mr. Raleigh's circle.

"Perhaps my teacher at home?" he suggested.

He told them about Tremayne.

"Will he do it?" Mr. Raleigh asked.

"I think so, sir."

"Why?"

"Because he is all for England in America."

Mr. Raleigh smiled, then he narrowed his eyes.

"Do you trust him with your life?"

"Yes."

"Is his manner courtly?"

"As courtly as mine."

"Courtly enough, then!" said Mr. Raleigh with a friendly laugh. "Write your teacher that you need to see him. Your message must be something only he will understand. Do not sign it. I'll read it before you write it final in the onion ink. You must assume now that everything we write here is read by others as soon as it leaves Durham House."

Andrew warmed at the prospect of being sent

back to Plymouth on a secret mission. He pictured some of his old schoolmates seeing him in Mr. Raleigh's livery. He imagined letting out a hint of what he was about.

"What shall I say when I see Mr. Tremayne?" he asked.

"You will ask in my name if he will help us get the map.

"You will say nothing of this to anyone," he added. "No one here, no one at home, is that clear?"

"Yes, sir," the boy said, looking down, sure that Mr. Raleigh had read his mind.

"You will travel in your country clothes."

As Andrew was leaving, Mr. Raleigh called after him, "You will tell Peter and William I am sending you back because you are homesick."

Andrew stopped like he'd been smacked.

"That last I don't like, sir," he said more quickly than was polite.

Mr. Raleigh gave him a sharp look. "You make bold to say so!"

Andrew stood silent as Mr. Raleigh glowered.

"You don't like telling the others?" he asked.

Andrew nodded.

The man's look softened. "I have pretended much and done many things I didn't like," he said. "I'm not asking of you a tenth part of what it took me to get here. You don't like wearing a mask? That's all I'm asking—that you wear a mask.

"Disguising is part of our work. Masks hide our purposes. In what we are about it's dangerous for anyone extra to know who we are or what our business is. So we go in disguise. Do you understand now?"

Andrew nodded slightly.

"Tell me," Mr. Raleigh asked, "have you ever met a stutterer?"

"Yes. One of my schoolfellows."

"Did you notice he was not afflicted when singing or acting a part?"

Andrew thought for a moment. It was true.

"Yes."

Mr. Raleigh opened his hands. "You'll find it is the same with you. Some tasks are easier if you do them playing at being someone else.

"It's like laughing when shamed. I hear you do that well. You have it in you to be one of my actors. Go play your part!"

Andrew half-smiled to himself as he left. He liked it that Mr. Raleigh thought he had it in him to be one of his actors. He could pretend homesickness as an actor. That wouldn't hurt his pride.

He went to his desk and wrote Tremayne: "Pray

meet at my cross midday Wednesday next. Yours for Eden."

That the note was from Andrew and what they were to meet about, Tremayne would figure from the mention of Eden. With Andrew's name in mind, he'd know their meeting place to be St. Andrew's Church.

Mr. Raleigh nodded when he read it.

"Good. Now copy it in the onion ink. It may even puzzle the Spanish ambassador. He's their chief spy here."

Andrew turned to leave.

"Wait!" Mr. Raleigh called. "I want to try your nose once more.

"What's this?" he asked, pushing a vial of black liquid to the boy's face.

Andrew sniffed and jerked back. It smelled like strong tar. It made his eyes water.

"Naphtha of the Persians," Mr. Raleigh said with a grim smile. "Now match the glasses again."

Andrew couldn't. He couldn't smell anything.

Mr. Raleigh smiled a tight smile as he nodded. "Watch that no one does that to you again. Your sense will return. The naphtha numbed it."

He poured some into a dish and struck a spark. Andrew jumped back as the liquid burst into flame with a thick smoke.

"Useful for mischief, if mischief is required," Mr. Raleigh said quietly. "Monsieur Pena and I once escaped a trap with it. As the Frenchmen crept up to slit our throats, we gave them a splash of naphtha and set them on fire."

Andrew walked slowly back to the dormitory, imagining Frenchmen with drawn knives in the shadows. At the window, sunlight burned like naphtha.

15

A VISIT HOME

That night in the dormitory, Andrew told William loud enough to awaken Peter, "I'm being sent back tomorrow because I'm homesick."

Somehow saying his lines as an actor and not as himself was easy.

He could tell, watching William's face, his friend guessed something was up. "Will you return?" William asked.

"I don't know."

Peter giggled. It was an ugly sound. Andrew lay in bed thinking to choke him.

The next morning, Mr. Harriot gave him money for his trip and a black band to tie around his right arm above the elbow.

"Folks will assume you are in mourning. Be grave," he said with a wink.

The boy rode hard. He wore the black band and kept to himself where he fed and rested. There were few questions.

The sea wind was sharp against him as he rode down to the coast from Exeter. By the time he reached Plymouth, it was blowing a gale with a fine stinging rain.

He stabled his mount and climbed the twisting narrow stone-paved lanes up to St. Andrew's Church. The few folks out were muffled against the weather.

He slipped into the church. It was like a huge upside-down ship, dark and silent. It smelled of soap and candles. The gloom was like a mist. He didn't see Tremayne. Had he got the message? Had someone given him the tincture to read it?

He could hardly breathe. Every sound made him jump. Then a shape he recognized slipped around a corner in the shadows and signaled with his hand.

They didn't speak. They walked apart, like strangers, down to the water's edge, bent deep into the wind.

"How did you read my message?" Andrew asked as they crouched under an overhang.

"A merry peddler calling himself Quinch came to my school singing and selling tonics," Tremayne said. "Only he was no peddler and what he sold me was no tonic. He was strange-looking and dirty—a small streaked face stuck on top of a ragbag body stuffed to bursting with layers of old sweaters over shirts and jackets. You couldn't tell what was belly and what was wrapping. He stank of onions; he looked like an onion! He grinned and burbled like a man drunk under his striped pack.

"I was about to turn him away when he half sang in his funny voice, 'I have something needful from your young friend's master.'

"I took him aside," Tremayne continued. "The man's eyes were honest. What made his face look strange were the streaks of soot and red clay he'd smeared on.

"Once we were out of earshot, he fumbled in his pack for a jar.

"'This will help you read something that's coming,' the fellow said, grinning and capering all the while as if he were presenting me with a great joke. I thought him mad, but he hinted enough to make me trust him. As he took my coin, he told me the trick of pouring the potion on the page. But what a smell as the sheet dried before the candle! And then the writing vanished!

"Some potion!" laughed Tremayne. "I hear he called at Stillwell too.

"So what's all this about?" he asked.

"Mr. Raleigh needs us to go to France, pretending we're wine merchants," Andrew explained. "Or rather, you are. I'm to be your clerk. At Marseilles we'll visit a man who deals in wines. He has a map Mr. Raleigh wants. We'll take it."

Tremayne's mouth sagged open as Andrew spoke. When the boy finished, his teacher shook his head slowly.

"I knew when you went up to London you'd come back with something for me—but this? A plot for two West Country folk to sneak to France and steal a merchant's papers? And what's he ever done to us? And what if we're caught?"

He made his eyes wide and formed his hands in the gesture of hanging.

"Yes! I'm in!" he said with a broad smile.

They agreed to meet a few days later at Durham House.

On his way back up to London, Andrew stopped at Stillwell.

It was noon. The dogs' greeting made him smile. His folks were just sitting down to dinner. "Andrew!" they yelled as one when he came in. For a moment he couldn't speak. If there were tears in the rush of hugs, no one noticed.

"Give us news!" his mother called as she bustled to set a place for him. "We have suet pudding—your favorite!"

He told what he could as he ate fast. Then he pushed his chair back, wiping his mouth on his sleeve. "I was ordered to hurry," he said.

"Yes!" they cried as he stood up. "Godspeed! Goodbye!"

He stopped at Rebecca's. She wore the red ribbon she'd bought with Doctor Dee's halfpenny. She laughed when he gave her the silk his silver toothpick had come wrapped in. It was the only thing on his person that had any connection with Mr. Raleigh. He'd ordered the boy to travel so spare that, even if he were stripped naked and everything about him were studied, there would be no link to Durham House.

16

PREPARATIONS FOR FRANCE

Andrew sat with Mr. Raleigh, Mr. Harriot, and Pena in the turret, waiting for Tremayne. The boy was jumpy. Despite the heat, his hands were cold when James knocked at the door.

"Yes!" called Mr. Raleigh. With him that word was never a question, always a statement.

"It's the one what's come for that one," said James, winking and pointing at Andrew as he pushed open the door.

As Tremayne stepped in, Andrew saw his teacher through Mr. Raleigh's eyes—a wiry brown-haired man, dusty and sweat-streaked, in plain clothes. He didn't look like a gentleman.

Mr. Harriot stood up to make him welcome. Tremayne was as squat and plain as Mr. Harriot was tall and elegant.

"I've heard about your time at Cambridge," Mr. Raleigh said after a long stare. "There is report that one Sunday a certain clergyman there preached against your teacher's politics. A few days later, a donkey was led up the stairs to the clergyman's rooms and given strong medicine. The beast was found in its mess with a sign around its neck: 'An ass purged of its foolishness.'

"Did you have anything to do with that?"

"Perhaps," said Tremayne. His face gave nothing away.

Andrew was anxious for his friend, but Tremayne was cool and easy.

"Your teacher—Mr. Eden—is reported to have a great interest in Spanish discoveries. Perhaps he has Catholic sympathies as well. Do you share them?"

"Perhaps." Again, not a flicker.

"So perhaps your interest in America is to see a Catholic colony there?"

"Perhaps."

Mr. Raleigh smiled. "Then perhaps you will do for us."

They proceeded to talk over small cakes and cups of Mr. Raleigh's cacao drink as Andrew sat silent beside them.

At dusk James announced, "Mr. Hakluyt."

Andrew was startled. He knew that name! Mr. Hakluyt's book was his bible.

A tall, gaunt man stooped through the doorway. His face was long and narrow, with overhanging brows. There was high color in his cheeks.

"Mr. Hakluyt is chaplain to our ambassador at Paris," Mr. Raleigh said, introducing him. "It was he who sent us news of the Frenchman's map. It must be one of the few he has not seen.

"Mr. Harriot you know," he told Mr. Hakluyt. "The gentleman next to him is our wine merchant in training, Mr. Tremayne."

Tremayne smiled and bowed.

"I know your book, sir," Tremayne said. "*Divers Voyages Touching the Discoverie of America.* I've taught my students from it—including that one," he said, pointing to Andrew.

"That sometime student is now our wine merchant's clerk," said Mr. Raleigh. "He has the nose."

Mr. Hakluyt was older than Mr. Raleigh. He looked like a hungry preacher, large-eyed and drawn.

He looked at Andrew and asked, "Do you know why we need that map?"

"Because you're going to America, sir," the boy answered.

"Well, some of us are," Mr. Hakluyt replied, studying him.

"Like nothing else, a map can show where you've been, where you are, and where you're going—where England's going. Geography is the eye of history."

He spoke in a deep slow voice like a Bible prophet.

"Give me a true map and I can master the world!" he said, his eyes boring into Andrew's.

The way he talked and what he said made the boy's scalp tingle.

"Here is Marseilles," said Mr. Raleigh, spreading out a chart and pointing to the main French port on the Mediterranean.

"With Andrew along as his clerk," Mr. Raleigh continued, "Tremayne will go there in disguise as a junior in the firm of Barnes and Barry, London wine merchants. He will call on the Frenchman and take his documents.

"Let your consciences be easy," Mr. Raleigh said. "The French have stolen many of ours. You two will even the score a little."

"His name is Réné Viton," said Mr. Hakluyt. "His home and place of business are on a hill overlooking the port. He is in his late fifties. Your firm has done business with his for years.

"Our London wine folks know nothing of this, but you, Tremayne, will carry their credential. Andrew will carry samples of the wines you're offering to trade for furs."

"And a vial of the opium tincture," Mr. Raleigh added.

"You will carry nothing to connect you with me or anyone at Court," Mr. Raleigh continued. "If you're caught, we'll not be able to help you. Whatever you say of us under torture, we will deny.

"Those are the terms. Will you do it?"

Tremayne looked at Andrew. Suddenly they weren't teacher and student anymore, they were like brothers, and, just like brothers about to take on something dangerous together, they began to laugh the helpless laughter that dispels fear.

For a moment everyone in the room laughed.

"Starting now, Andrew, you'll pitch your voice lower," Mr. Hakluyt ordered. "And touch a bit of charcoal to your upper lip. Not much, just a hint of what is to come. It will make you more likely."

He tested their French and taught them something about the wine trade. For days he and Pena lived with Andrew and Tremayne in rooms apart from the others, all their speech in French as they made up conversations about wines and furs and acted out meeting men on the docks who might help them.

In disguise, Tremayne and Andrew visited Barnes & Barry to study their people and their goods. The boy wore a touch of charcoal. He sweated; it smeared.

As part of their education, they learned the names and qualities of a dozen vintages. Then Mr. Raleigh arranged for them to get smuggled into Barnes & Barry's huge wine vault one night to see how such goods are stored and the measures of pipes, barrels, kegs, and casks. There were spirits enough down there to souse all London, and the air was so close, so dizzyingly sweet, so fumed with alcohol, Andrew and Tremayne got faint-headed. It was all they could do to get out.

"This is for you," Mr. Hakluyt said the next day as he handed Andrew a worn Barnes & Barry horsehide samples case. Inside were six small bottles of wine.

"And now to Mistress Witkens," Mr. Raleigh announced.

She was bent over her bench, back to the door, when they all crowded into her workroom.

"Mistress Witkens!" Mr. Raleigh yelled. "Mistress Witkens!"

She turned and rose slowly, snatching up her white bag cap. As she pulled it on crooked, she beamed and made to curtsy.

"What's the honor I owe your visit to, sir?" she hollered, studying Mr. Raleigh's face to read his lips.

Mr. Raleigh bowed. "We need vests for these lads," he said in a high loud voice. "Vests."

"Vests?" she bellowed, narrowing her eyes. "Vests? Vests in summer?" She scrunched up her face and shook her head.

"Waxed-canvas vests," Mr. Raleigh hollered, moving close to her. He spoke slowly. "Canvas vests lined with silk they will wear under their shirts, silk side to the body. Each will have a large pocket at the front. No straps or buttons—they will sew them tight themselves when they put them on. They'll sew the pockets shut when they're filled."

He gestured how wide the pocket should be—the width of their chests.

With that, she nodded and began to hum as she measured and scribbled notes.

"What will they be putting in 'em?" she asked.

"No need for you to know that!" Mr. Raleigh snapped.

117

"I need to know for depth of gusset, Master! Depth of gusset. Gussets and vents bulk things up."

Mr. Raleigh showed with his hands how much the vests should open out—enough for a thin book.

"Put everything else aside. Make them up as quickly as you can!"

As they returned to the turret, Mr. Hakluyt explained about the vests. "You'll slip the documents into the pockets, sew them shut, then sew the vests tight around your bodies. You will find the needles and waxed thread you need in the pockets."

"Now for the drug, Andrew," Mr. Raleigh said when they got to his room. "I will teach you how to handle it.

"You will flourish your napkin like this, pretending to wipe clean the glass before you pour the sample. With the vial of potion hidden in its folds, you will tap a single drop into the Frenchman's glass.

"Just so! Now you do it."

Andrew's hand shook so hard he emptied the vial all at once.

"Deep breaths," Mr. Raleigh said. "Take deep breaths."

The boy practiced until he could do it with his eyes shut, one drop at a time.

"You will carry six drops," Mr. Raleigh said. "Never taste it."

It is like poison, the boy thought as he pinched his lips together. *I'll be giving the Frenchman poison.*

17

TO MARSEILLES

"To throw off folks curious about where you are going," Mr. Raleigh said, "your route to Marseilles must not be direct."

He handed Tremayne and Andrew lumps of root about the size of an acorn.

"Ginger root from the Orient. We buy it from Arab traders and take it from Spanish prizes. When you feel seasick, chew on it. It will burn your tongue, but take as much as you can. Your stomach will be grateful. Save what's left like you'd guard a jewel. When your guts churn, there's nothing more precious."

Slouching around the London docks in worn country clothes like an idle worker, Tremayne bought them passage on a small ship calling at Lisbon. It would then slip through the Strait of Gibraltar into the

Mediterranean and tack up the coast of Spain to France and Marseilles.

"She sails tomorrow on the change of tide," Tremayne reported when he got back. "She's an old cog, not much bigger than this room, freighted with dried fish from Newfoundland. The corsairs won't bother her."

"Corsairs?" Andrew asked.

"Pirates from Barbary and Algiers. They lurk around the Strait and the Canary Islands. Their spies at the ports alert them to vessels loading rich cargoes and passengers worth a ransom."

"Pirates?" Andrew gasped. "Pirates will be after us?"

"Don't worry," laughed Tremayne. "You and me and a cargo of stockfish don't offer much opportunity. But a fleet for America? That would tempt them."

"What are stockfish?" the boy asked.

"Gutted cod dried in the air until they're like boards. All the juice goes out, just the stink remains. The Spaniards use it like dried meat—soak it soft and cook it in their stews."

The ship did smell of fish, but it was clean, and the crewmen were friendly. "Passengers are a bonus for them," Tremayne explained. "What we pay will get shared around, a bit for everyone."

Andrew hadn't been on a big ship before. The sails creaked and ropes whistled as the cog rocked and shuddered in weather, groaning with every wave. He could hear the "clank clank clank" as men worked the pumps. He began to feel queasy. The fish smell didn't help his stomach. After a few hours, the two passengers smelled like the cargo. Andrew bit on the ginger root. It was stringy and hot in his mouth. He wasn't as sick as he'd been on the Thames ferries.

They laid over in Lisbon, trading fish for spices, wines, and oil. Andrew stood by the captain, watching this business closely, amazed when the captain told him what he'd sell his new cargo for in London compared to what he'd paid for the fish he gave in exchange.

"You're surprised, lad? Well, don't you be thinking our profits come easy. We pay in life for risks of weather, raiders, and ship fever before a penny makes it to our pockets. There's more sailors under the water this moment than on it!"

Once they set out again, the cog felt sturdy underfoot. Andrew liked the compactness of things on board. No space was wasted; there was nothing extra, yet everything needed was close at hand. It was like Mr. Raleigh's room in the turret.

Andrew stood by the captain at the wheel as they approached the Strait through the Gulf of Cádiz. A dark, unmarked vessel approached quickly, then drifted off.

"A corsair out hunting," said the captain. "She must have caught smell of us."

From the crew, Tremayne bought two suits of sailors' clothes, worn and not too fresh. He and Andrew put them on.

"The prison." Tremayne pointed as their ship eased past the immense pink stone fortifications guarding Marseilles harbor. Château d'If was a fort on its own dark island, with sharp black rocks poking out from the rough water around it. The two spies looked at each other; each knew what the other was thinking.

They landed in their sailors' clothes, people of no class, kind, or nation. They smelled of old fish. No one noticed them.

The harbor's edge was a hive packed tight with people of all colors, women yelling over their tables of writhing fish and piles of spiked shells, men trundling goods to and from warehouses along narrow ways in rattling iron-wheeled carts. There were rare smells from the open stalls for vegetables, spices, dried fruits, nuts. The voices were loud, high-pitched, excited.

It was late July. The sun was piercing. The hills were parched, oatmeal colored, speckled with dark green pines. The breeze was sharp with pine.

They found the avenue they'd been directed to. A whiff of goat roasting with rosemary drew them like dogs to an open-front tavern that looked clean enough. They ate the cook's one offering. In the place for necessaries out back, they changed into their merchant clothes. Andrew touched charcoal to his upper lip.

A little farther on they found an inn. They arranged their lodging and left their sailor clothes and the samples case in their room.

They called at Monsieur Viton's with their credential. A black giant opened the door. The name Barnes & Barry on the paper gained them entrance. It was cool and still inside.

"The French use stone like English builders use wood and paint," Tremayne murmured as they waited. Andrew looked around. The walls were of colored marble up to the height of a man's head. The white stone stairway was as broad as a farm road. Overhead there were painted scenes: blue skies, naked figures, flowers, eagles. They stood beside a great tub of polished tan stone mounted on black carvings of lions' paws.

"It's large enough for a man to lie down in, isn't

it?" Tremayne whispered. "And you know what? A man *did* lie down in it, a dead man in ancient times. It's a tomb, a sarcophagus, which means 'flesh-eating stone.' Keep out of it if you can," he added as he widened his eyes and grinned.

Andrew was too scared to like his joke.

At last Viton appeared, short and strong, with thick black hair and eyebrows and small, tired eyes. His nose was veined, his face puffy.

He was reserved in the way a man aware of his station is with those he knows to be inferior.

"But why was I not advised of your coming and some appointment made?" the Monsieur asked, squinting as if he could not quite make them out. "And who is this boy?"

He stared hard at Andrew.

Andrew figured he must have sweated off the charcoal.

Tremayne apologized. He pointed to the credential the Monsieur was holding. "I understood my principal, Mr. Douglas, wrote to you some weeks ago. His message must have gone astray. As for the lad, he is my clerk and my nose."

Viton said nothing. The two visitors had not been invited to move from where they stood.

Tremayne's face grew red. "Sir," he said in a soft

way, "the firm of Barnes and Barry intends no rude-ness. We shall withdraw and proceed to Palermo, or you will accept proof that we are who we say we are and allow us to present our merchandise and see yours."

"What proof?" the Monsieur asked.

"The nose of a vintner. Present your tests and the lad will match them. He has the gift."

The Monsieur peered at them in turn from head to toe.

"It is most unusual. But come," he said after a pause. "My man Brion will bring refreshment and samples to try your clerk's nose."

To the left there were large double doors to the room that served as Viton & Frères's countinghouse. Viton led them to the right, into a long hall. The floors were of polished stone set with smaller stones in fig-ures and patterns. In London, Andrew had seen the like in places where wealthy Romans had lived a thou-sand years before.

Brion brought a pitcher of sweetened lemon water and a dozen small glasses for the clerk to match.

Andrew caught his breath as Brion presented the first. Pretending to sneeze, he knocked it over. The stuff spilled on Brion's sleeve. It was naphtha.

Andrew pushed himself away, apologizing as he wiped his nose. He'd saved it.

The Monsieur pressed his lips together as Andrew moved to the other side of the table.

Viton's samples were easy to sort and match, easier than those Mr. Raleigh had used for his test.

Over the lemon water, Tremayne went through his rehearsed lines about samples and furs.

Andrew was edgy as he thought about what was coming. At last Tremayne suggested that since they were fatigued from traveling and the heat, perhaps they could meet for supper.

"Yes," said the Monsieur. "I will look for you at the change of bells."

Back at their inn they bathed and sewed each other into the vests. The vests were hot and uncomfortable and gave the small black biting creatures of that region safe harbor next to the wearers' skins. Again Andrew applied the charcoal.

He felt in his inner pocket for the drug vial. His hand shook when he touched it. *Poison!* he thought. *I may kill him!* He forced himself to take deep breaths. Despite the heat, he had goose bumps.

18

ADVENTURE IN THE WINE TRADE

At the change of bells, Brion admitted them. His large smooth face revealed nothing. Viton was there with his clerk, a sturdy fellow, heavier and taller than Tremayne. Andrew caught himself feeling for the dagger strapped to his thigh. If it came to violence, they were outmatched.

Over dinner, the Monsieur and Tremayne discussed their voyage from Lisbon, prices of wines there, fashions in London, and the Englishman's interest in furs. Andrew sat silent, eating little. He wondered if the food was poisoned.

"And your Mr. Parmenter," the Frenchman asked suddenly. "How is his health?"

Andrew felt the blood go out of his body. He'd not heard that name in connection with Barnes & Barry. Tremayne took it for a test.

"I am not acquainted with Mr. Parmenter," he replied in an easy voice.

"In your firm, Mr. Parmenter?"

"No, I am not aware of such a person."

"Um," said Viton, pursing his lips.

Andrew had tensed for a fight. He let himself sink back in the chair.

"May we now offer our samples and discuss an exchange?" Tremayne asked.

"Yes."

Andrew opened the samples case. Brion set six glasses before him and put a bowl in front of Viton. Viton's clerk sat beside him. Brion remained standing.

Andrew's heart was pounding. He fought to take deep breaths as he arranged the six small bottles on the table. He had the vial in his pocket.

As he had practiced with Mr. Raleigh so many times, he took up his napkin to polish the first glass and slipped the vial into his hand.

With the vial concealed in the napkin's folds, he dosed the glass as he poured the sample. He sniffed it and said what it was in his deepest voice.

Tremayne took a list from his pocket. "Yes," he said pompously. "This is our finest Canary. We have five barrels available."

"You try it first," said the Monsieur to Tremayne.

Andrew handed Tremayne the glass, turning it carefully as he passed it. They had trained for this. The drug was heavier than the wine. It would settle to the bottom if not stirred.

Tremayne sniffed deeply, took a sip, ran it around in his mouth, then swallowed. "Ah! Most excellent," he said, smacking his lips. "How can we hope to replace such wares at the exchange we are willing to let it go for?" he mused.

The Monsieur flashed a greedy look as Tremayne swirled the glass, pretending to savor its fragrance one last time before passing it on.

The Monsieur sniffed, took a taste, then spat.

He closed his eyes for an instant and nodded. "Yes," he said. "We would be interested in that."

He passed the glass to his clerk. The clerk did as his master had done.

They were not as thirsty as Mr. Raleigh had thought they'd be. Andrew would have to dose the next glass as well.

"The second," said Tremayne.

Andrew's strength was back. Again he flourished the napkin and tapped the vial.

Again the Frenchman sniffed, worked the wine around in his mouth, and spat.

He and Tremayne had some conversation about this one, then about the third and the fourth. The clerk and Andrew were kept busy making notes as Brion looked on.

Andrew had two drops left.

The Frenchman was becoming more agreeable. Perhaps he was getting some of the drug. He directed Brion and the clerk to go fetch samples of his furs for Tremayne to judge.

"As you go, take those," he said, pointing to the glasses he'd tasted from.

Brion gathered them and left the room. The clerk followed.

Waiting for the others to return, Tremayne drew the Frenchman out about his trade and the prices of furs.

"I don't know what's keeping them," the Monsieur said finally. "Of course they are polishing off the samples, but still . . ."

Andrew forced himself not to look at Tremayne.

"Well," said the Monsieur, with a wave of his hand. "Let's try number five."

Again Andrew prepared the glass, sniffed it, and announced what it was as he passed it to Tremayne, who sniffed and tasted, then swallowed with a grunt of satisfaction. He passed the glass on to Viton with a friendly nod. Perhaps he was getting some of the drug too?

The Monsieur sniffed, smiled, and drank it down.

"That one also—it will do," he said. "Make a note."

As Andrew did so, Viton rang his bell.

Silence.

"Ah!" he said thickly. "Well, the last, and then I'll fetch my drunkards."

The boy flourished the napkin one last time and emptied the vial.

Viton swallowed it all. The man was a horse or the potion was water.

He rang again.

Silence.

He started to heave himself up.

"Oof!" he exclaimed as his legs went out. He sat down hard. With a long sigh, he sank forward on the table.

Andrew kept his eyes down.

The Frenchman snored deeply.

"Now!" whispered Tremayne.

They went out the way Brion and the clerk had gone. The two lay sprawled in the pantry. They'd drained the glasses.

Andrew snatched up their candles.

"The cook," Tremayne said, gesturing that they should pass through the kitchen. The place was silent. They came to a door. Andrew opened it without a sound. The cook was asleep inside. He took the key. As he turned it from the outside, the lock screeched. He went cold all over. They waited. She slept on.

They hurried to the Monsieur's apartment. They searched until the bells rang half past ten. There were folders and folios and sheaves of letters tied with ribbon but nothing resembling the map and the other papers Mr. Hakluyt had described.

Suddenly they heard "thump" and what sounded like a cry.

Andrew grabbed his dagger.

It was the Monsieur's large old tabby cat, glad for company.

As Andrew petted her and his heart slowed down, Tremayne asked in an everyday voice, "If you were the Monsieur, where would you hide those documents?"

On an inspiration Andrew said, "Out in the open, as if they were ordinary things of business. Not here, not where thieves would look for valuables."

They went back down past their sleepers and on to the room in front where Viton & Frères conducted their business. What appeared to be the map they were after was with some other papers in a folio marked "Trades Current." There wasn't light enough to be sure.

The boy's hands shook as he stuffed part of the file into the pocket of Tremayne's vest. Tremayne then did the same for Andrew. Tremayne's hands were cold. Their shirts were stretched tight.

"And the samples case?" Andrew asked.

"Leave it," said Tremayne. "We've got enough to carry."

They slipped back through the kitchen and out the rear door into the alley.

No one was around.

They made their way to the inn, dodging through the harbor warren to make sure no one was following.

As they sewed the vests shut, Tremayne said, "We can't stay. We must ship out tonight."

They changed into their sailors' clothes, paid the startled innkeeper, and slipped into the street.

At that hour there were men of opportunity about, willing—for a price—to do anything.

In a tavern by the water, they found a Dutch sailor who told them his vessel was headed to Lisbon on the change of tide. Tremayne bought his favor and he smuggled them aboard. By dawn, Marseilles and its prison island were out of sight.

19

REPORT TO MR. RALEIGH

Word of their return got to Durham House before they'd anchored in the Pool. Pena and Mr. Harriot met them at the dock. At the great door of Mr. Raleigh's house, James was waiting for them, beaming. They hurried up to the turret, where Mr. Harriot cut the vests away. The skin underneath was red and oozing from bugs and chafing.

Mr. Raleigh wrapped them in towels and rang for James.

"Tell the kitchen to send a boy with a bucket of warm water and a stack of clean cloths from the laundry. Quick!"

While they waited, Tremayne made everyone laugh by telling how Brion had tested Andrew with naphtha and Viton had made Tremayne try the first sample. He told how the noisy lock to the cook's door had made Andrew jump and how the cat's yowl had made him do the same.

Mr. Raleigh washed their sores. The soap and water stung. Then he rummaged in his sea chest.

"I'm going to put on medicine," he told Andrew. "It will burn, but you'll have no scars. Hold him, Monsieur Pena!"

Pena held the boy tight. Suddenly his sores burned like flares. Andrew lurched and bit his lip bloody to keep from crying out. Then the hurts went numb.

When it was Tremayne's turn, Mr. Raleigh gave him a rag to put in his mouth to keep from cursing. When the medicine hit him, Tremayne whipped about like a caught fish.

Mr. Raleigh cut open the vest pockets. All eyes were on him as he sorted through the papers.

"You did well," he said. "You got the map."

He pointed to it. "Did you look?"

"No," said Tremayne. "There wasn't time."

"Look now," said Mr. Raleigh. "The West Indian islands are shown with their harbors. Where the Spaniards have forts, there are red marks."

He paused and looked at Tremayne.

"Will you go with them?" he asked. The sweep of his hand took in Mr. Harriot and Andrew.

"The three of us?" Tremayne asked. "Andrew, Mr. Harriot, and me?"

"Yes," said Mr. Raleigh. "You three are my Americans now."

Andrew caught his breath: he was going too! Pena was nodding and smiling at him.

"Yes, I'll go," said Tremayne.

"Good," said Mr. Raleigh. "Understand, you'll not be going as settlers: this expedition will be to gather facts and write a report to encourage others to invest and settle. You and Andrew will go as explorers under Mr. Harriot.

"For now, go back to your school and carry on as before. We hope to sail in the spring.

"Neither of you will speak of this to anyone. To those who ask, say you've been to Ireland."

He nodded for them to leave.

As Andrew got to the door, he turned and asked the question that had been gnawing at him since the night they left Marseilles.

"Sir, did the drug kill them?"

"No," Mr. Raleigh said with a dry laugh. "I diluted it to one-quarter strength. I feared your hand would shake and you'd give too much."

"So they're alive?"

"Ha!" he exclaimed, making a face. "They are,

and eager to renew your acquaintance, along with the Crown's agents who have warrants for your arrest. Had you not made it out that night, you might not be standing here. By dawn they were searching every ship.

"That map you took—it did not belong to Viton, you know. He'd borrowed it from someone high in Paris who had no business lending it.

"Trouble all around!" Mr. Raleigh said with a happy smile.

When Andrew got into the hall, Pena embraced him.

"The French have invitations for me too," he said. His face was grim.

"For you? Why?"

"We were plotting against the Crown," he said.

"The gardeners?" Andrew asked.

"In life we all wear many hats," he said slowly. "To some I was a gardener, to others I was a revolutionary for the Protestant cause. My name was on their list. A dozen years ago on Saint Bartholomew's Eve, they killed ten thousand of us Protestants. All of my family. Every Huguenot on which they could lay their hands— noble or simple, man, woman, or child—murdered. The streets ran with blood; the river was full of corpses. The killing went on for days as Catholics rose in many towns and followed the example of Paris.

"Mr. Raleigh was in France then," Pena continued. "We were escaping together when we got caught. The men who found us had their knives out to cut our throats when Mr. Raleigh splashed them with his black oil and set them afire.

"Ah!" he exclaimed, shaking the dark memory from his mind like a dog shedding water.

"Come see our children!" said Pena. "The plants, the seedlings—the melons are up! And today we begin the swimming!"

"No!" cried Andrew.

"Well, when your sores heal."

That night, Andrew undressed out of sight. He was so tired he left his clothes where they fell.

"Where have you been?" William asked.

"To Ireland, training to be a merchant."

"You would be a merchant?" Peter sneered. "Only that?"

Peter's tone of voice made him shiver, like the scraping of fingernails over slate.

"That much," Andrew replied quietly. It crossed his mind to tell them what Doctor Dee had said about merchants being heirs to adventure, but he didn't. He was too tired.

Hours later he awakened to Peter's shrieks: "A Catholic! Andrew is a Catholic! A spy!"

Somehow, when Andrew undressed, the rosary Rebecca had given him must have slipped from his pocket. When Peter got up in the night, he'd found it.

As William and Andrew started up, Peter dashed into the hall, yelling, "Andrew is a spy! Andrew is a spy!"

For a moment the boy lay helpless. Then his strength came on, like pouring naphtha on a going fire. He dashed into the hall and tackled Peter front-on, head to gut, taking him down hard and knocking his wind out. Peter was heavier and stronger, but at that moment his kicks and heavings were like a fly's flutterings to the younger boy's fury.

With his teeth, Andrew shredded his nightshirt and tied Peter at the elbows as tight as he could. Peter was screaming a different tune now as Andrew half-rose and sat down on him hard to knock his wind out again. Peter lay still, gasping like a beached fish.

He tied Peter's legs together at the knees, then his ankles to his hands. The senior page ended up writhing like a trussed pig, gibbering and crying.

Andrew stood over him. The beads lay next to the wall.

By now William was there, along with Mr. Harriot, Pena, and James. Andrew wiped blood from his nose.

Andrew looked at them, then at Peter. "You tell them," he panted.

He picked up the beads and went back to bed. As he lay down, he figured that was it for him at Durham House. He wasn't sorry. It was like a boil burst: whatever followed, the relief was worth it. He went to sleep and slept wonderfully.

The next morning Peter and Andrew stood before Mr. Raleigh. Andrew's head throbbed. Peter could hardly walk.

Mr. Raleigh's face was like carved stone.

"Show me," he said.

Andrew pulled the beads from his pocket.

Mr. Raleigh shook his head like one annoyed at something small. "Put them away and go to your work."

The next day, Peter left for Ireland.

Some weeks later, Mr. Barnes and Mr. Barry received a thundering letter from Viton & Frères accusing them of sponsoring common thieves. As proof, they returned the worn Barnes & Barry leather samples case, the six small bottles safe in their lamb's-wool compartments.

20

THE SWIMMING LESSON

"Today is for the swimming!" Pena announced. "The sailors say to respect the sea you must never learn to swim, because if you do she will take you as one of her own. To that I say, *'Zut!'*" He spat.

It was a warm afternoon. The tide was flowing. The water moved like a huge brown snake, hissing as it pushed and frothed past Mr. Raleigh's water gate. It smelled of dead plants, old rope, rot, dead fish. Andrew's skin crawled at the thought of going in, but Pena was determined.

They took off their clothes. The steps were moss covered and slippery. Pena went into the water ahead of Andrew. It was cold. It grabbed at the boy's knees as he balanced on the last step.

"Fall toward me now," Pena ordered. "I will catch you."

A surge of water knocked Andrew in. He coughed and thrashed as the burly Frenchman made to hold him. He felt himself going down. He couldn't breathe. The panic of drowning gripped him like a bear crushing its victim.

"Easy! Easy!" the Frenchman yelled. "You are not so heavy in the water! Now you will lie on your back. I will hold you up. Lie still!"

Andrew couldn't. He was howling and flailing, shivering from cold and fear as Pena half-lifted him and turned him over. The boy's legs and hands were churning and kicking. He couldn't help himself.

"No need! No need!" Pena yelled. His hands were under Andrew's back. "You see, you float, *non*?"

"No!" Andrew screamed. "No! No!"

"Draw your breath and arch your back. Let your hands and feet flutter," the Frenchman yelled. "Now you float! You do not sink! Look!"

Laughing, Pena held up his hands. Andrew was almost floating as he gagged and spat out mouthfuls of the awful water. He was struggling, choking, screaming. But he got the trick of it.

Pena showed him how he could lie steady in the water by flapping his feet and making half circles with his open hands. With Pena's help, he made it back to the stairs. He was shaking. His feet slipped. He fell back and went under, swallowing a mouthful.

As Andrew retched and gasped, Pena pushed him onto the worn steps.

"Now fall in on your own and roll over," Pena ordered.

Andrew hesitated. Pena pulled him in.

"Now kick like the duck," the man said. "Let your feet work like ducks' feet."

He used a small log floating by to buoy his student as he kicked. Andrew was able to get back to the steps on his own.

They clambered out.

Pena made Andrew stand over the cistern again, cold and miserable, his stomach heaving.

"Observe the frog," the man said as he dropped a frog into the tank. "Watch how he pulls himself forward with his fronts as he kicks with his rears. You see how he positions his rear legs, drawing them up, out, and in together.

"You will do this now. I will hold you. Back into the water."

They practiced until the skin on Andrew's fingers was puffy and wrinkled.

"You do not want to paddle like a dog," Pena said. "That is too tiring. The way a frog swims, he can rest as he goes. So can you, with the turning over on your back.

"Give a dog a long distance to swim and he will drown, which is how geese and ducks defend themselves—they let the dog get close and then paddle on, drawing him out and out, and then, *voilà*! No dog!

"Today perhaps I save your life."

21

APPEAL TO THE QUEEN

It was a warm afternoon. The air was sweet with blossoms and the first downed leaves. Durham House was mirrored in the river.

Andrew was working with Pena, harvesting some of their Spanish seedlings, trying to figure out what they might be good for.

"First we crush a leaf and a root for smell," said Pena. "Some of these I know as herbs for seasoning. Too bad we keep no goat here: she could tell us what's good to eat. A cow, even better; the cow is a more delicate feeder," Pena explained.

"Ah! This is good," Pena said, holding up a root. "Ginger. And this one, sarsaparilla. They flavor their drinks with it. But these—" he said, waving his hand over a pile of wilting plants, "I can make nothing of them. Next year their blooms and fruits will tell us more, yes?

"There is a tree I look for," he said. "I hear the Indians in New Spain treat fever with the bark of a tree—but what tree?"

On his way to bathe, Andrew met Mr. Harriot in the hall.

"Mr. Raleigh's just summoned Mr. Hakluyt and your friend Tremayne to come help write an appeal to the Queen to let our expedition sail."

"I thought she was for it," Andrew said.

"It hangs in the balance. Her advisors fear war with Spain if we go; for her part, she frets at the expense. Many hands reach out; few realize how little she has to give.

"'When people arrive at my age,' she said sourly to Mr. Raleigh, 'they take all they can get with both hands and only give with the little finger.'

"'Your little finger, madam,' he replied, 'will do very well for us!'

"She smiled at that—a good sign. Now we must persuade her to twitch that finger in our favor."

When the others arrived, Andrew was called to the turret. Mr. Raleigh's writing board was awash with books, maps, and papers.

"Arrange that mess under three trumpets," Mr. Hakluyt ordered. "'Riches,' 'Faith,' and 'Safety.' Our Queen loves those horns best, so we're going to blow her such a tune she'll dance her way to the New World!

"The first—the loudest—will play to her nose for riches. People in the colony will send her strings of pearls, and perhaps there is gold. We'll hint but make no promise.

"We *can* promise profit in the trade as those people buy our English products and provide the things we now trade with others for—sugar, silk, and emeralds.

"Our second trumpet will proclaim her chance to bring Reformed Religion to the natives—gentler and kinder than what the Catholic Spaniards practice. They rob and murder their natives and torture to convert; ours will be the true Christian way.

"The third—the trumpet Safety—will announce a place for vagrants, petty criminals, and enclosure men.

"Do you know about enclosure men?" he asked.

"I do," Andrew muttered. His tone made Mr. Hakluyt look up.

"Good," he said drily. "Few at Court seem to.

"Once you've got our papers arranged, you'll write as Mr. Harriot, Pena, and Tremayne direct—a list

149

of everything the expedition will require. The Queen is England's frugal housewife. She'll want to know the quantity and price of everything. Check your addition carefully, for she will!"

Andrew wrote as the men directed—so many kegs of nails, so many shovels and axes, so many barrels of flour and stockfish, two hundred wool hats, five hundred blankets. They worked for days going over old expedition records and provisioning logs.

"But what about toys?" Andrew asked suddenly.

"Toys?" Tremayne and Mr. Harriot exclaimed together. "We're taking no children. What will the explorers want with toys?"

"We've got gifts for the chiefs and grown people we meet," Andrew answered. "We'll want to make their children our friends too. Tops and puzzles, dolls to dress, whistles, toy animals on wheels with strings to pull, hobbyhorses . . ."

"But they don't know horses—or pigs or cattle, for that matter," Tremayne said.

Pena looked at Andrew and nodded. "Yes," he said thoughtfully. "The children might become our first friends and bring the others along."

"Perhaps," said Mr. Harriot after a pause. "Add toys to the list."

The next day, they finished drafting and polishing. Their appeal to the Queen—including the list of supplies and toys—ran sixty-three pages.

Tremayne hurried back to Plymouth.

William was called to help Andrew write the final copies. Their backs and necks ached as their fingers stained black with ink and the fine sand they used for drying got up their noses and in their hair. They both had cuts where their penknives slipped as they sharpened the quills.

Mr. Raleigh composed the title page: "A Discourse of Western Planting: Certain reasons to induce Her Majesty and the State to take in hand the western voyage and the planting therein."

That afternoon, he and Mr. Hakluyt went to Whitehall Palace to present their appeal to the Queen. Mr. Harriot went along in case she had questions about what the explorers might require.

Late in the day, against all orders for secrecy, in his high excitement Mr. Harriot sent a messenger from the palace with a note for Andrew:

"It goes! The Queen adventures the ship *Tyger* and four hundred pounds of the Irish spice—gunpowder from the Tower. More, she lends her name. In an inspiration of flattery, Mr. Raleigh proposed naming the place 'Virginia' after her celebrated condition. It is said she smiled, so it is allowed. With her name attached, the colony is more than his venture, it is hers as well, and indeed all England's. In her pleasure he is now Sir Walter. He has ordered a seal struck with new arms and title, 'Sir Walter Raleigh, Lord and Governor of Virginia.' Her Lord Treasurer fought against it all until the Queen in fury told him, 'I have been strong enough to lift you out of the dirt, and I am still able to cast you down again.'

"Burn this."

Andrew's hands shook as he folded the note into his pocket. He didn't burn it. In his excitement he forgot what that news might mean to the Spaniards. He forgot all about Sir Walter's orders for secrecy. He couldn't stand still! He had to tell someone! That night, he sent Mr. Harriot's note on to his father with this scribbled on the outside: "We're going to Virginia! Get this to Tremayne!"

Days later, Andrew was dirty and sweating, hoeing squashes with Pena, when he was ordered to the turret. There was no time to wash or change.

Mr. Harriot was there, ghastly pale, rubbing his hands together, his eyes wide when they met Andrew's. Sir Walter was darker than the boy had ever seen him.

"Where is it?" Sir Walter demanded.

Andrew knew what he meant. His weakness clutched at his chest. He had difficulty getting breath.

"What, sir?" he stammered at last.

"The letter Mr. Harriot sent you."

A lie flickered. It died on the boy's tongue.

"I sent it home," he panted.

"So you did," said Sir Walter, holding up a sheet of paper, "and here's the copy made by a Spanish agent at Plymouth. Interesting reading for the Spaniards!

"Why did you do this against my orders?"

All was over anyway. Andrew spoke his heart, even though it was pounding so hard he thought it would jump out of his chest.

"Pride, sir. Pride in what we'd done persuading the Queen."

Sir Walter gave him a long look. "'Pride goeth before a fall' is the maxim," he muttered.

Andrew stood straight, his eyes held to Mr. Raleigh's as he waited to hear him say, "Go!"

Mr. Raleigh turned away and walked to the window. "Of course they knew it already," he said. "But out of pride you might someday give them the bit they don't have, the piece that works as the key.

"Maybe now you will believe how good their taps are, how thoroughly we are watched.

"Enough," he muttered. "You both spoke truly. You're valuable to the cause. Get back to it, but study to be quiet. And, Andrew," he added, "this shortness of breath you suffer. It is like your blush. Every actor knows it. When you feel it coming, force yourself to breathe deep before you speak."

22

THE WELL

Late that fall there were record tides on the Thames. The well at Durham House turned brackish. Sir Walter ordered his engineers to dig it deeper.

Pena and Andrew were working in the orchard mulching fruit trees. The well was fifty yards away, as large around as a stout man. The engineers were working in shifts, one pumping with a bilge pump, one at the bottom digging and putting his spoil in a bucket, which another raised and lowered when the digger tugged at his line. The fourth man worked perched above the digger, sealing the stonework with mortar. It was dank, dark work.

Andrew didn't like tight places. It made him giddy to look down that hole.

Suddenly he felt the earth tremble. There was a rumbling noise, then shouts. The well had caved! The men on top were hauling the sealer out, his head gushing blood. The bottom-most man was trapped, and the narrowed hole was filling with water. The engineers were rushing about, screaming for help.

"Reset your pipes!" Pena ordered. "Pump! Pump hard!"

He looked at Andrew. "No one else is thin enough to get down. You must go see if he is alive. If he is, dig him out!"

"Me?" Andrew whispered. He had no voice.

"You!" roared Pena. "Be quick!"

The boy was lowered in harness with a trowel. The spoils bucket followed overhead. As he sank into darkness, he struggled to gulp air.

The man below him was stuck in a weight of clay and stone. Andrew could hear his groans, but it was too dark to make out his face.

"I . . . can't . . . breathe," the man panted. "My chest, my shoulder . . ."

"Courage!" Andrew called. He was acting now, playing at being someone else, someone brave.

"Courage!" the man gasped as Andrew reached him and began scraping away the mass at his chest. The man's right arm was twisted at an odd angle.

For hours the boy dug and loaded stone and wet clay. The space was so close he could make only small movements. His arms grew numb, but the cheers from above that greeted every bucket he sent up inspired his working.

The men on top lowered mugs of beer in the empty spoils bucket. The pumpers kept the water down.

At last the man was clear almost to his waist, but he was still in too deep for the men above to draw him out without tearing his joints. It had gone from dark to black in the hole.

Suddenly a small circle of warm orange light staggered down. The light revealed Andrew and the trapped man to each other for the first time. They tried to smile at each other through sweat and grime. Mr. Harriot had ordered a fire built and rigged his mirrors and lenses to cast a beam. It was not large, but it was everything.

When Andrew had cleared the man to his knees, he gave the signal that they should try to lift him. The man screamed as the rope pulled at his hurts. The muck gave him up with an ugly sucking noise. As they hoisted Andrew clear, he followed.

Mr. Harriot helped unhitch Andrew's harness and wrapped him in a blanket. After seeing to the engineer, Sir Walter joined them.

"Will he be all right?" Andrew asked.

"I snapped his shoulder back in place," Sir Walter

said. "He's bruised and cut, but, yes, he'll be all right. I gave him a drop of Doctor Dee's opium tincture to ease his pain. He's sleeping now."

He gave Andrew a long look. "I was sixteen when I first killed a man," he said slowly. "I was twenty before I saved one. You're earlier at saving."

"Your father once saved me from drowning. Did you know that?"

"Yes, sir."

Sir Walter nodded. "You do well keeping to yourself. Few learn to. Mr. Harriot has remarked that about you.

"He says he needs your help getting ready for Virginia and writing his reports when he gets there. We all know about his writing, so I've agreed you may serve him as secretary, beginning now. In Virginia you will go with him everywhere he goes and write as he directs—gathering notes for our advertisement for Virginia. He'll pay you a wage and supply your kit."

Sir Walter must have noticed a change in Andrew's face.

"Your work for him as secretary counts for more than being my page," he said gently. "Do you understand that?"

"Yes . . . sir," Andrew stammered. How could he explain that while he was glad for the promotion, Sir

Walter was the man he admired most in the world and he didn't want to leave his service?

He didn't need to explain. Sir Walter smiled and gave him a friendly pat. "We'll do things together again when you get back. I promise!"

23

THE TWO INDIANS

Late that night Mr. Harriot came to the dormitory and shook Andrew awake.

"Sir Walter calls us," he whispered, his voice charged. "It's the exploring captains to America. They've arrived with two Indians!"

William heard. He sat up and waved as Andrew went out.

James was lighting torches in the main hall, where sailors trundled in crates and trunks. Sir Walter's turret was bright with candles. The two sailing captains, dressed in their best silks, sat beside Sir Walter. Two Indians wearing deerskin capes squatted on the bare floor. They were not tied. There were no guards.

As he slipped in behind Mr. Harriot, Andrew caught the eye of the closer Indian. There was worry and curiosity in it, but no fear.

"We found a secret island, thick with trees and overgrown with grapes," the older captain was saying. "The people are gentle and so eager to trade; one copper pot buys ten fine deerskins. They have pearls," he said, handing a string to Sir Walter.

"The chief we met wore it to show his wealth and power. We traded a small copper kettle to get it for the Queen."

"Large as berries, they are," Sir Walter said as he weighed it. "This will please her—pearls are her favorite jewel. But go on—the island . . ."

"Roanoke is well hidden, with rough shallows all around," the man continued. "We left a fort for your use—a frame of wood and earth behind a good ditch."

Andrew barely heard as he stared at the Indians. They sat motionless. They looked to be about eighteen, the color of rubbed bronze. Their heads were shaved clean, save for a ridge of stiff black hair that ran from forehead to neck. They were well muscled, not tall. Were they prisoners?

Their eyes were on Sir Walter. Their stares drew his.

"Mr. Harriot, you and Andrew will learn their language," he ordered. "See to their comforts as you help them understand how we live. Ask what they find strange. Ask every question you can think of: Is there gold? Do they know a way to the Pacific Sea? What do they eat? What are their medicines? What is their religion? Learn about their people, how they live. Andrew will write down their answers."

Andrew looked over at Mr. Harriot as the tall man raised his eyebrows. The boy looked back at the Indians. Did they have any idea what was being said?

"To my ear their tongue is ugly," the younger captain muttered, shaking his head, "and you'll find it harder than any Spanish code. Most of our talking has been pointing and grunting."

"What do they need?" Sir Walter asked.

"They eat ship biscuit and salt pork," the man replied. "Bread, meat from the spit. Give them water, no ale—they do not brew in Virginia, so it makes them sick. They sleep in their deerskins on reed mats from their country. You'll find them restless; they'll want lots of exercise.

"They keep strong drugs in the leather pouches at their waists for ceremonies. One they stuff up their noses, the other they sprinkle a pinch of on an open fire and sniff up the smoke. It makes them drunk, so when they do that, be careful."

Mr. Harriot said he knew the smoke drug. The Spanish called it tobacco.

"We won't leave them on their own," Sir Walter said. "They'll live in the apartment next to Mr. Harriot's. He and Andrew will be their daytime companions. We'll keep some of our people around them always."

William was awake when Andrew returned.

"What are they like?" he whispered.

"I don't know," Andrew replied in a hushed voice. "I couldn't tell if they were frightened or pleased at being here. The captains say they volunteered to come, though for what pay or reward I don't know."

"Are they tied?" William asked.

"No, but they're to be kept close. Mr. Harriot and I are to stay with them and study their ways. The captains say their voices are high for singing their prayers; to each other they grunt low. They talk little."

"What do they look like?"

"They're brick colored," Andrew whispered as he got into bed. "Their heads are shaved so there's just a strip down the middle. Manteo is the handsomer. He has high cheekbones. The captains say he is the higher born, the son of a great priest. The other, Wanchese, has a dark look. Their fingernails are long, like claws, for fighting. Sir Walter says Mr. Harriot and I must learn their language."

"And shave your head?" William murmured as he turned away.

The boys had just gone back to sleep when there were thumps and shouts from the hall. They rushed out. There was smoke! The Indians' room was on fire!

They'd raked coals from the fireplace out onto the floor to smoke their drug. "I went in when I smelled burning," the man minding them explained. "They was singing, whooping and dancing, and when I come in to check, they pitch me out to my hurt!"

Andrew and Mr. Harriot settled them, then went back to bed as the Indians' minder settled grumbling in his chair.

"Get us some of their drug to try!" William said. He giggled.

"I don't think they did it for pleasure," Andrew said. "I didn't see tears, but I think they were crying."

As they followed the Indians around the next day, Andrew asked Mr. Harriot, "Why did they come?"

"I'm told the captains showed them many strange things," the tall man said quietly, "talked about saving their souls and promised to make them powerful chiefs when they returned. They gave them Bibles, crosses, knives, and trinkets. The Indians were dazzled. They had no idea what they were getting into. When they lost sight of land, they lay on the deck moaning and singing to their god."

The strange-looking pair attracted crowds. People came up to touch them. When a well-dressed lady did so, Wanchese reached for her brooch. As she pushed his hand away, he tore the jewel from her blouse and pinned it to his cape. A moment later, Manteo lifted off a man's hat and put it on. It sank down over his ears. When the man tried to take it back, he got knocked down.

"Make a record," Sir Walter laughed when he heard. "I'll pay for their hats and jewels. Those two are walking advertisements for my Virginia colony!"

"Advertisements?" Andrew asked.

"Proof to the common people that there really is a New World out there," Mr. Raleigh explained. "Some will want to go see where they came from."

Andrew wondered what the warriors thought about being paraded around.

"They aren't shackled like the trained bears that dance outside Whitehall Palace with rings through their noses," he said to Mr. Harriot later, "but they're being used the same way. It's wrong!"

Mr. Harriot pursed his lips as he thought.

"No," he said at last, shaking his head. "They're learning about us, how we live. They'll go back and tell the others. When we go to their country and they show us around, we will be the curiosities poked and stared at. They'll have to care for us just as we care for them, protecting us from things we have no idea of. There is no other way."

That night, Andrew dreamed he was in an Algonquin camp, feeling as strange as Manteo and Wanchese must have felt in London. Dark people stared and pointed at him. He understood nothing he heard; the food they offered tasted strange. He was ignorant of everything, locked out of words. The strangeness of it all worked like one of Mr. Harriot's glasses, magnifying his loneliness.

24

CHRISTMAS REVELS

The Queen ordered Sir Walter to bring the Indians to Whitehall Palace for her Christmas Revels. Andrew and Mr. Harriot had learned some of their Algonquin language by now, so they went along as interpreters.

Andrew stood tall, proud to enter the Presence Room of the palace in his best page's outfit: tan hose, pale gray tunic with "WR" embroidered in red silk at the center, black shoes of Venetian leather. Mr. Harriot wore what he always wore, his long black coat.

The great hall was bright with music, scented candles, and cords of evergreens. The people wore perfume and powder. The air was choking thick with cinnamon, clove, sweat, and smoke.

There were great platters of meat cut up small for the guests to spear on their knives, pies and sugared fruits, marchpane, sweetmeats, and great bowls of syllabub—thick cream mixed with sweet wine, lemon rinds, and sugar. One cup made Andrew's head spin. The company downed it like water.

Sir Walter wore the orange silk tunic of the Queen's Guard over black hose, his knife at his belt. A gold hoop flashed in his ear. He looked the prince of pirates.

On a sign from Raleigh, Andrew and Mr. Harriot paraded the Indians forward, their bodies oiled and painted mulberry red under their war costumes—loincloths, ornamented deerskin capes, and the stone-headed war hatchets they called tomahawks. As they walked, they gestured what they would do to their enemies. It was not pretend; despite everything Andrew and Mr. Harriot had said to put them at ease, they lived ready to fight.

The revelers stilled and murmured as the two glided past.

Manteo and Wanchese understood that while Sir Walter was chief of Durham House, the Queen was Big Chief Elizabeth, in charge of all.

To a drum-and-trumpet fanfare of Sir Walter's composing, the Indians were to carry the boar's head to the Queen's table—red water like blood at the neck, its tusks and eyes wetted so it would appear fresh killed.

It was Andrew's first visit to the Queen. She took no notice of him; she saw only the warriors. Her eyes were brown and piercing, coldly measuring everything she saw.

As Andrew stood to one side, he tried to figure her age. Was she as old as or older than his mother? Her body was that of a youngish woman, but her face was a puzzle. It was long and pointed. Her chin was sharp. *It could be a boy's face,* he thought. *She is not beautiful, but she looks strong in purpose.*

To appear young, Elizabeth had her people smear her face with a fine white paste that concealed every blemish. Behind this mask, only her eyes and mouth moved, her mouth but little. The heavy jeweled dress and jacket she wore kept her body fixed in place.

The Indians had a superstition that the paleness of their English skin meant they were spirits from the dead. The whiteness of the Queen's face scared them. In Virginia, when a chief died, they dressed him in his finery and laid him on a shelf in a special house they kept for their dead.

That moment in the Presence Room, Manteo and Wanchese thought they were in the presence of a dead chief who moved her eyes and hands!

The Indians forgot to bend the knee as taught. Manteo crept forward like one stalking game, staring at the Queen's hands. She was proud of her hands. She had beautiful slender fingers adorned with many rings. When she noticed Manteo's staring, she twiddled her fingers a little to show them better.

Andrew froze as Manteo reached to touch her hands, Wanchese crouching up close behind. No one was permitted to touch the Queen except at her bidding!

Her guards rushed forward. Wanchese raised his war hatchet. Mr. Harriot and Andrew stepped before them as Sir Walter and others in the company pushed the guards back.

"No hurt! No hurt!" the Queen laughed. She'd taken it all as flattery. She might not have been so flattered had she known what the Indians thought they were seeing.

Manteo pointed to her earring and signaled he wished to put it in his ear.

Mr. Harriot explained the Indians' gift custom. "Among their leading people, when one admires something, the other is expected to make a present of it. You must give it to him," he said.

The Queen glowered. "Must? Is 'must' a word to be addressed to princes?"

Manteo smiled and nodded as if he'd understood all. The Queen shook her head and summoned one of her ladies to remove the ornament. The Indian jammed the pointed end of the earring into the rim of his ear. Blood dripped from the stab, but he seemed not to notice.

Andrew watched, wide-eyed, sure that he and his charges were going to get in trouble for so much forwardness with the Queen. No. She turned away with a laugh to greet the ambassadors. Manteo touched his ear and smiled at Andrew.

After the banquet there was music and dancing. The Queen changed her gown for the dancing. She did not like to eat in front of people, but she loved to dance for an audience.

To a roll of kettledrums and trumpets, she reappeared in a costume of striped black and white silk figured with pearls.

Sir Walter had changed too. His costume was almost the match.

The Queen started when she saw it; then she laughed and took him up. To her, all was flattery.

She led the dancing with Sir Walter on her arm. The gentlemen and ladies of Court followed in rows and squares of dancers.

Horns, tambourines, drums, lutes, trumpets, and

flutes played in the great hall under flickering orange-and-yellow flames. One of the women wore crushed garnet in her hair so it sparkled red like flashes of fire. Other heads in that light glittered with green of emerald dust; some were touched with blue of ground lapis.

Two were dusted with gold. None was dressed so fine as the Queen, though.

She led the pavane, fine figured and graceful, pointing her feet exactly, turning like a leaf spinning in air. One by one her partners dropped away as she danced on alone, faster and faster.

Suddenly she stopped and summoned her maids to lift off her jacket and blouse. Her breasts bared, she resumed as before, only now with her hands over her head.

Andrew's mouth went dry. Never in all the gossip about the Queen had he heard about this! He looked at Mr. Harriot. The man stared openmouthed.

Manteo and Wanchese stared breathless and openmouthed too at this dead-god chief of chiefs. Did she mean to cast some fantastic spell on them?

They whispered to each other as they snuffed up pinches of drug from the pouches at their belts. Then, in frenzy, they rushed the musicians. Manteo seized a drum; Wanchese went for a tambourine.

The music stopped, and with it the Queen's dance as the Indians began their own music before her, banging drum and tambourine and howling so loud and heartfelt it seemed their throats would tear.

Pouring sweat, they danced and cried to save their

lives. Then, as if on some silent signal, they quit and dashed out into the cold.

The company thought it all a show and cheered as Andrew ran after them, calling, desperate, sure they were going to kill themselves. He found them by the river. Mr. Harriot came up, out of breath. The Indians would not take the coats they offered. They would not speak. The four walked together, silent, back to Durham House.

25

TO AMSTERDAM

Just before Christmas there was a hard frost. Pena and Andrew had bedded the gardens for winter and wrapped the more tender fruit trees. All fall they'd battled slugs, snails, rats, and moles.

"Moles work at night mostly," Pena had explained, "but if you see one tunneling, you must dig him out with care and be gentle how you kill him. His skin is fine for caps."

Now, with the wind biting mean, he gave Andrew one he'd stitched himself from four mole pelts. It was soft as velvet.

"You will wear it, yes? Fur side to the head. The others will not have such caps! Let them taste the cold! This is your cap for America!"

It was a dull gray day, but Andrew was merry: he was going home for Christmas. Mr. Harriot was

176

headed to Amsterdam to buy instruments and see to the making of lenses for use in Virginia. From the instrument makers he hoped to learn about the new astronomical discoveries.

An hour before the coach left for Exeter, Andrew was summoned to the turret—to exchange Christmas wishes with Sir Walter, he thought.

Mr. Harriot was there. His mouth was tight. He shook his head when Andrew came in, then looked down.

"You must go to Amsterdam tonight in Mr. Harriot's stead," Sir Walter announced. He was grim-faced. His tone was flat. "The Queen demands Mr. Harriot's presence at Whitehall to show our Indians again and do his frightening tricks for the Turk emissaries. His warriors and the fire snakes have gained him reputation!"

"I was promised a holiday," Andrew blurted in his dismay. "I have plans."

"Mind your tongue!" barked Sir Walter. "We all had plans. You will do as I order. Go!"

"Don't be angry with Sir Walter," Mr. Harriot muttered as they went down the stairs. "This is all useless bother to him, and he has the Queen's wrath coming. He told her the Indians will not dance again. 'Order them in my name and they will!' she said.

"They won't, and following the broil sure to come I must present fire toys for her guests, among them the foreign agents and ambassadors who would have my throat slit if they could. You know what mischief they arranged for Doctor Dee. . . ."

When they got to his room, Mr. Harriot handed Andrew the glass slugs to be ground into lenses.

"You'll manage them," he said. It wasn't a question. He'd taught Andrew to measure the correct pitch from the Arab's book.

Mr. Harriot drew a paper from the pocket of his black cloak. "You will call on the instrument makers there for me and collect what they've made. They all live in one quarter of the city, but they're hard to find. If you locate one and earn his trust, he'll direct you to the next, and he in turn will pass you on. Guard this paper. In the wrong hands it could cause hurt."

"Is their work secret?" Andrew asked.

"There are some who think even clock makers work for the devil, so those artisans live quiet," Mr. Harriot said, looking away and frowning. "Some of them know the new science. Much of that is secret: how the stars move, the planets, the moons. It is not what the Church teaches. Such news always makes men afraid.

"You forfeit a holiday with your parents," he said. "I lose a chance to hear about discoveries in the heavens made by a Pole named Copernicus—all to parade two men who deserve better than to be trotted about like circus animals."

He fumbled again in his deep pocket. "The name of the vessel I was to ship on," he said as he handed Andrew a scrap. "You'll board her below London Bridge at high tide. You will wear my disguise."

"Disguise?" Andrew asked.

"Yes. You will go in the dress I was planning to wear—as a Catholic woman fleeing England."

"But how will I get word to my people?" Andrew asked. "And to Rebecca—how can I let her know I'm not coming?"

"Sir Walter has seen to that," Mr. Harriot said. "As we speak, the peddler who took Doctor Dee's reading tincture to your people is awaiting your place on the Exeter coach."

Mr. Harriot gave Andrew two small bags, one of slugs, the other of gold. "Those people are honest," he said. "Pay what they ask."

Dark comes early around Christmas. No one was about as Andrew stepped into the Strand in the disguise of a religious woman.

In blowing drizzle and a thick fog, he made his way to London Bridge and down the flight of stone steps to Irongate Wharf. There was a smell of fish. His ship lay at anchor. He made his way down the gangway. Instead of Pena's moleskin cap, he wore a wimple, a nun's hat. His bust was filled out with wads of wool that itched and tickled. His holy book was Mr. Harriot's Arab book of optics. Under his skirts he carried the gold and slugs. He had to walk slowly to muffle what was tied about his waist.

The crossing was rough. It rained and sleeted on the Channel, the wind shrieking and snarling in the rigging like spirits. The ship creaked and groaned like she was dying. The trip was all staggering up steep hills of frothing waves and falling down the other side, only to begin the same again as waves dashed and slobbered them. They made nothing forward; it was all side to side.

Andrew stayed on deck. He knew he'd be sick below.

As he chewed his ginger, the crew pumped in shifts like galley slaves. They called to him.

"Who do you send your prayers through, Sister?"

"Saint Nicholas!" Andrew yelled as loud as he could in his false voice.

They cheered. Saint Nicholas was the patron saint of seamen and children in their helplessness. They were helpless, but slowly, after hours of deluge, the gray paled and the sea calmed enough for the pumps to get ahead of the flood down below.

They dropped anchor in the Hook of Holland. Snow mixed with drizzle as Andrew rode overland to Rotterdam and Gouda and on to Amsterdam. The buildings were not so fine as London's. Outside the towns, everything was flat and white with windmill after windmill. His diet on the road was dark bread, dark beer, onions, and cheese. His mood was black.

Even without the bags strapped to him, it was difficult going about in a long dress. He stumbled on stairs. Strangers greeted him in the street and asked particulars of his holy life. He kept a small stone under his tongue and feigned to be mute, as Sir Walter had instructed.

With some difficulty, he found Mr. Harriot's jeweler. The Jew and his family spoke English. They made Andrew welcome with a warm room and a decent meal.

While the man worked at his kick wheel, shaping and polishing the lenses, Andrew ran Mr. Harriot's other errands. At night he measured each lens against what was given in the Arab's book.

He stayed with the jeweler's family over Christmas, struggling to talk high, eat dainty, and hold his legs and arms like a woman. Out of respect for his nun's dress, they called him Sister. His voice was changing, cracking like William's. He made to cough when that happened.

If the jeweler and his family suspected his disguise, they never let on. They were used to sheltering people hiding who they were, where they were from, what their business was. It was everywhere a time of war, watchfulness, and secrets.

Along with their Torah, the jeweler had the Bible in English in Mr. Tyndale's translation. Andrew was used to hearing readings from Saint Luke on Christmas Eve. Instead, on this Christmas Eve, the jeweler and his wife and their children took turns reading aloud the story of the Jews' exodus from Egypt.

"Our family story is the same," the jeweler told Andrew as the last candles died. "Our people fled Spain the year Columbus sailed for the New World. By decree of May 1492, all Jews were given four months to choose between leaving the country without any valuables or embracing the Catholic faith. Eighty thousand left, our people among them."

"And now, here, are you safe?" Andrew asked.

"Some people are never safe," the jeweler replied. It was too dark to make out his face.

They heard singing in the street, faint at first, then swelling louder and louder. "Come," said the jeweler, opening the door. "They are the Star Singers, the town poor out caroling. It is the one time in the year they are allowed to gather."

A mob filled the road, motley and ragged, young and old, some carrying candle lanterns. At the head of their procession, a stout man, a kind of giant, carried a large star on a pole. "The star in its stable of light," he chanted in Dutch between the songs, "the star in its stable of light."

Andrew thrilled to their music. He'd never heard anything like it—so many voices in such a space, hopeful, joyful. It was better than any church singing.

A child came up. "Alms, please, alms," she begged. Andrew figured her meaning.

As he fumbled for money, the jeweler gave her a coin. Then Andrew came up with his.

"Christ bless you both and your house all," the child said with a curtsy.

"And you and yours," the jeweler replied as he closed the door.

Sir Walter had sent Andrew off with a note to open on Christmas Eve. When he was alone that night, he did:

"Andrew—I send you Christmas blessing. The enclosed is for yours at home." It was signed "WR."

"The enclosed" was a small gold coin, the one they called an angel. Sir Walter meant it for Rebecca.

26

To Virginia

It was early on a spring morning. Andrew stood waiting for Pena by the door of Durham House in rough clothes and his cap for America, and a rat catcher out calling his trade in the Strand took him for a servant.

"Hey, lad! A brave dog here," he yelled. "Good company! Keep you free of varmints!"

The furry pup squirmed in the man's rough hand. The rat catcher laughed and came close. "Tuck him in your jacket, boy. My terrier just littered. This one's the runt. No use to me, but he'll be good for you. Lad your age needs a dog," he said, slipping the pup into the boy's pocket. "See? He fits!"

Andrew curled his hand gently around the warm wriggle as Pena walked up.

"Ah, you've got a friend close by now," the

Frenchman laughed. He rubbed the small white muzzle. The puppy licked his finger.

"It's salt he's after," Pena said, nodding. The puppy continued licking as fast as he could. "Salt of the earth, salt of the sea," Pena murmured.

"So I'll call him Salt!" Andrew exclaimed as Pena handed the rat catcher a small coin.

William was at his desk when Andrew came in later. As he looked up, Salt crawled free and fell to the floor with a squeal. He piddled, then limped to William and pawed his shoe.

"Ah," said William, gathering up the dog and making small noises. "Your protector in America."

At the start of their time together, Salt lived in Andrew's jacket. The boy liked the dog's smell and the comforting noises he made at night when he snuggled beside Andrew's head.

At last, after all the preparing, packing and repacking, corking tight the bottle of naphtha, polishing and oiling the edge tools until their blades gleamed like silver, checking lenses, astrolabes, and sundials, greasing vests, belts, and boots with a mixture of turpentine, beeswax, and boiled sheep's fat against weathers they could only imagine, after counting out buttons, beads, bells, and toys—how many would they need? Would a hundred of each be enough?—in early April, word came that the ships were ready.

Andrew was working in his room, making up a kit for Tremayne, when Mr. Harriot came in.

"There's word at Court," he said, "that Plymouth's taverns are full of our explorers filling every ear with tales of gold and adventure. They are as set on piracy as exploring."

"We go as pirates?" Andrew asked with a start.

"We'll take prizes as we go. Our explorers count on catching a fat Spanish merchant ship or two on the way. It's the same with Sir Walter and his investors: gold on land and gold at sea is what they're after."

He was looking at the box of mirrors.

"Should we make them presents of those?" he asked. "They might be used against us for signaling or blinding."

"How?" asked the boy, surprised.

"Watch," said Mr. Harriot as he rose and went to the window. Early-spring sunlight was pouring in. He took one of the mirrors and, with a sureness that showed his practice, flashed a blinding beam into Andrew's face.

"The Greeks used that trick against the Romans two thousand years ago," Mr. Harriot said. "With sheets of polished bronze, they beamed sunlight on the

Romans' ships and set them afire. Good weapons, mirrors. Not to be given away."

"Right!" said Andrew, blinking and rubbing his eyes.

The next morning, with Salt in his pocket, Andrew set out for Plymouth with Mr. Harriot. James stood with Mistress Witkens, William, the cooks, and the laundry people at the door to cheer them off.

Andrew's breath came short as he waved goodbye to his Durham House friends. His face was hot. He swallowed a lot. After Pena, he knew he'd miss William most of all.

Slowly, though, the word "Virginia" began to drum in his head as he rode, the rhythm of the hoofbeats repeating it.

Even in the hot spring sunshine, Mr. Harriot, riding alongside, wore his long black cloak with the deep pocket.

Manteo and Wanchese had gone ahead with Pena and Sir Walter. "You're going home," Andrew had explained to the Indians. "Home. Back," he'd said, pointing. "Over the great water."

"Home!" the Indians had repeated, smiling. "Home!"

Andrew met his parents and Rebecca above the port at Plymouth Castle. Words came hard; nobody knew what to say. The boy was excited and distracted.

It felt like getting ready for a footrace: all he could think about, all he wanted, was to be off, to go! Down below, the Virginia fleet looked like toys, with toy people milling about and waving flags as horns and kettledrums played a popular battle march. There was no secret about their business now; everyone knew they were bound for America—but where exactly?

At last it was time for farewells. He gave his parents and Rebecca awkward hugs. "I'll write," he promised.

He hurried down to join the expedition people. Tremayne was there, looking over the kit Andrew had made for him. Pena was holding two packages. "The apple shoots," he said sternly as he handed over the smaller one. "Put them in your coat and keep them damp. First thing when you land, plant them and water them good!" His face softened as he held out the second package. "We are brothers of the spade now," he said as he presented Andrew with a fine French shovel, the shaft and handle one piece of bent hickory, its heart-shaped blade the best steel. "With this one you will plant our English seeds and dig new things to bring home."

The man's face worked with feeling; Andrew's too.

Sir Walter came over. He stretched his arms around Mr. Harriot, Tremayne, and Andrew. "You're my Americans!" he said. "Observe everything! Be my eyes. Take in all." Then his face changed and he looked away to study the fleet—his fleet, if he'd had his way. His gaze went beyond the ships, beyond the harbor.

They were among the last to board. The gangplank went up behind them.

The fort's cannons boomed a farewell salute as trumpets blared the Queen's anthem. Then Admiral Grenville raised his arm and the sailors threw off the hawsers that bound the Virginia fleet to England.

As the ships moved out on the ebbing tide, something let go inside the boy. He couldn't help it; tears came as he waved and cheered, until all he could make out was the motion of Sir Walter swooping his feathered hat up and down.

27

A STORM AT SEA

With Salt in his pocket, Andrew spent his first days at sea exploring the *Tyger*. She was larger and newer than the cog he and Tremayne had taken to Marseilles. He clambered from hold to top deck, from stem to stern, marveling at all the spaces, every inch put to use. "When you spread it out deck by deck and add in the hold," he told Tremayne, "it's as big as Durham House, only the ceilings are low."

Admiral Grenville made no secret they were English. The *Tyger* flew St. George's great white cross on red with Sir Walter's pennant underneath as the fleet sailed down the French coast and out across the Bay of Biscay.

The admiral kept his ships close together in what he called his wolf pack. Close sailing was his special tactic. None of the vessels they saw at a distance dared approach. None of those carried flags.

The sailors watched the sky for signs of weather. They told its future in clouds and colors:

"Red skies at morning, sailors take warning;
Red skies at night, sailors' delight."

One morning it dawned red. Before noon the long strands of white cloud they'd had for days gave way to lead-colored masses ranked like fish scales. A softness came into the air. As Andrew came up from seeing to the Indians, a man called to him: "A gale's up, lad! Get set for damp and worse!"

Already the sky was darkening. The boy gritted his teeth against feeling afraid.

The weather turned fast as the wind shifted, blue water going to an ugly gray pudding, whipped and seething. Sudden gusts made the furled sails crack like gunshots. Wind with cold rain in it tore at the lines, making them snap and moan.

"You hear that?" the sailor said, coming close. "Voices of the drowned. Do you know the verse 'Full fathom five my father lies'? Do you hear them singing it now?"

Andrew heard. His flesh prickled. He forced himself to smile. It came hard.

"Look!" said the sailor, unbuttoning his shirt to show the medal he wore. "Saint Nicholas—the protector of sailors. Pray to him, boy! He'll save you!"

All the crew knew Saint Nicholas. Catholic, Protestant, Arab, and Jew—and there were some of each—prayed to him and felt better for it. Andrew had done so himself on the ship to Amsterdam; he did again.

He went down into the steamy, pitching, sweat-and-wet-smelling hold to join Tremayne in the galley, where the sailors drank beer and ate cold biscuit as they rested between watches and shifts at the pumps. There was no drying off.

As the waves grew steeper, the *Tyger* climbed and fell like a blind beetle going over rocks. The ship tossed and took on water. Andrew chewed ginger root. It did no good; he lost what he'd eaten.

Thunder boomed so loud he thought they'd run into a nest of Spaniards. Lightning flashes made the ropes glow white and sizzle. Water surged over the main deck. Salt lay buried in Andrew's bunk.

He went down to the hold to see Manteo and Wanchese. They clung to each other in their corner, sick and groaning, praying to a small, carved figure of their god.

"Ginger root!" Andrew said, handing them chunks. "Chew it to feel better." They wouldn't.

"It won't last long," he said, as much to himself as to them. "We'll be all right! You're going home."

They were too miserable to be cheered.

The smells and smoke in that tight place, the sight of swaying ropes and netting, the Indians being sick— it all got to Andrew. He began to feel faint. He staggered back up to the deck.

As he lurched out into the smack of rain, the small ship just ahead began to founder. The gale winds and pitching seas had cracked her spine! Smoke was pouring from the main hatch: she was on fire! After taking on water, there's no greater threat to a ship than fire.

"The heavings and tossings broke her cook fire loose!" a sailor yelled. "There's gunpowder in her! I helped load kegs of it!"

Tremayne and Mr. Harriot came and stood with Andrew, gripping the taffrail.

At risk of smashing the *Tyger* to bits or getting her blown out of the water, Admiral Grenville had his sailors work the few small sails he'd left up like they were butterfly wings, inching the flagship close to the pinnace.

Andrew, Tremayne, and Mr. Harriot helped feed rope to the crew as they heaved lines across and tied the pinnace to the larger ship. As side rails and scuppers ground to splinters, the pinnace crew jumped across.

Andrew could hear the fire roaring in her guts. Orange was showing at her hatches.

"That gunpowder could go any second," Tremayne muttered.

"Count!" the pinnace's captain yelled from her deck. "Get the count!" He wouldn't jump until he knew all his men were safe.

"There's courage!" Mr. Harriot yelled to Andrew, his lips pinched together as he watched.

Sure at last that his people were off, the pinnace captain took an ax to the ropes, then made the leap, the ship's cat in his arms, wet and furious.

Andrew was watching the pinnace. "She goes down like someone pulling the covers over," he murmured to himself. No one heard him. At that moment every man watching was beyond hearing, focused on the vessel's death agony.

She lurched up with a muffled boom when her powder caught. Andrew held the rail so tight his knuckles went white as the *Tyger* shuddered at the shock. Bits of board and blanket boiled up, then bubbles.

The *Tyger* was crowded now, with two crews aboard along with explorers and Indians. There was no sitting down for meals; everyone stood to eat and shared bunks.

"Always a warm bed to get to," the sailors laughed, one man crawling under the covers as another crawled out. Andrew and Tremayne shared with the Indians. The Indians would have shared with the sailors too, but those men were afraid, one muttering, "I'd sooner sleep standing up than lie down next to a heathen!"

"The admiral says there's food enough," Tremayne told Andrew, "but we'll soon be short of water and out of beer."

The storm that took the pinnace hung over them for days. They sailed in murk, seeing nothing. With charts and a sea compass, the admiral kept their course.

One morning Andrew, Tremayne, and Mr. Harriot stood together watching the admiral at his work. For Mr. Harriot, navigation was science; for Tremayne, it was a tool to be learned; for Andrew, it was magic, like Doctor Dee gazing into his crystal ball.

Even in clear weather the sea gave no hint of where they were. The magic and terror of open-water sailing was that there was no left or right, and they didn't even know if they were going straight.

With his astrolabe, the admiral checked their north-south position against the stars when he could see them again.

"We're about where we should be," he said, smiling, as Andrew and Tremayne watched him work.

"Another Arab invention for you, Andrew," said Mr. Harriot, pointing to the sea compass.

Mr. Harriot had never sailed out of sight of land before either. He began to understand some of the things the navigators he'd tutored at Durham House had found so puzzling. "Theory and practice," he muttered. "I was all theory, they were all practice. From now on I'm for practice."

"We're making for the Canaries," the admiral announced. "Off the coast of Africa. Spanish islands, the last land. There we'll take on fresh water and the fruits for scurvy—oranges and lemons."

"What's scurvy, sir?" Andrew asked. He'd heard Sir Walter speak of it.

"Sailors' sickness. Your gums go soft, the teeth loosen, every joint hurts, you bruise so much you look like a ragbag. So suck your lemon, lad, and give up whistling for an hour."

Andrew was with the admiral as they approached Tenerife. Two Spanish ships of war moved out from the harbor.

"You're in luck, lad!" the admiral exclaimed. "Maybe I can give you a bit of a sea fight!"

He aimed his wolf pack straight for the closest. She turned away. He went after the other. She too decided on other business.

"To keep from getting trapped in the harbor, we'll settle well out," the admiral explained once he gave the order to drop anchor. "We'll take the small boat in. I have a friend here, the principal merchant. You know," he said with a wink, "a man who buys much and pays in gold is always the intimate of merchants, whatever their differences in politics and religion.

"Just in case, though, my people will carry arms to assure a kind reception."

There was no need: the admiral's gift of brightly dyed English wool—the finest in the world—for the merchant's lady inspired the offer of a banquet.

"Oh, no!" said the admiral, bowing and opening his arms. "I could only accept if my entire company were invited, and that would be too much, for in addition to my special guests"—he beckoned, waving his arm at Andrew, Tremayne, and Mr. Harriot—"my crews and the other explorers number more than a hundred and fifty." He paused. "And we have two Indians in our party!"

"Bring all!" the Señor answered bravely. "I would not have it any other way! Pray, bring all, even your savages."

The admiral raised his hand in mock surrender. "So, Andrew," he laughed, "you see how it is with a Spanish gentleman!"

The gentleman's profits eased down gullets as crew, explorers, and Indians came ashore in shifts to eat roast ox and fresh greens and drink the famous wines of that place. The wine affected the Indians; they got giddy and fell asleep.

After he got over feeling he was still on a rocking boat, Andrew wanted to explore the island and hunt for seashells like the ones the sailors had shown him.

"No," said Mr. Harriot. "You and Tremayne must stay with the Indians. We can leave behind an explorer or a sailor, but it won't do to lose *them*! They're our Virginia navigators!"

The Señora had a small female dog she fanned as she held it to her bosom. When her dog spied Salt, it gave a bark of joy and leaped clear. The lady screamed, then hid her face behind her fan as the dogs tore off together, frisking, yipping, rolling, and rollicking. Only when Salt was tired and thirsty was Andrew able to catch him.

The admiral's people left in high spirits, with oranges and lemons and almost as many casks of their hosts' wine as their water.

Andrew went out in the last boat with Manteo and Wanchese. As they looked back, Manteo pointed. "Green, like home. Hot. Not like London."

The enemy's ships of war saw them off from a distance. As a courtesy, Admiral Grenville dipped the flagship's ensign. The Spaniards did the same. "Sailors don't hate each other the way soldiers do," the admiral said. "We have in common a more constant enemy: the sea."

Leaving the dark green Canaries behind, they sailed southwest along the coast of Africa until they picked up the equatorial current that flowed to the West Indies.

"Watch now!" the admiral said as he pointed to the compass. "We turn to follow the directions Columbus gave his mariners a hundred years ago:

"'West.

"West.

"Nothing to the North.

"Nothing to the South.

"West.'"

Andrew stood with the Indians and Tremayne. They felt the *Tyger* heel as she turned and left the Old World behind.

"Now we're really on our way," Tremayne cried, his eyes bright as he stared at the line where the western sky met the sea. "There!" he exclaimed, pointing and poking Andrew as he laughed with excitement. "Do you remember my telling you 'There sits America, waiting for you'? Well, there she is!"

Andrew nodded and laughed as a shiver of anticipation swept over him. The Indians smiled. They understood.

That night, the ship's wake glowed like moonlight as she cut through a swarm of tiny jellyfish.

The *Tyger* became the boy's world as he studied the mechanics of raising the heavy sails with lines run through block and tackle to multiply the crewmen's strength. He began to notice as sailors do slight shifts of wind and changes in the ship's creaking. He learned how it is that some men choose to be sailors for life as he worked with the ship's carpenters.

One day a carpenter held up a long, tapering piece of oak.

"Hi, boy! Do you know what this is?"

"A builder's peg, sir?"

"To a landsman. To a sailor it's a treenail: what fastens ship timbers one to another. We pare it to fit snug in a bored hole, bung it in, and then she goes to work on her own as the water swells her and she locks tighter and tighter. An iron spike would rust and work free. For building on your Virginia island, lad, treenails! From what I hear, it's plenty wet there."

Andrew tried to imagine what he'd find at Roanoke, what he'd build. His mind raced over the tools they'd packed. Had they brought everything they'd need?

28

PRIZES!

They sped west as Admiral Grenville crowded on sail.
The storms they met came up from behind and pushed
them on. They were not so violent as the one that
broke the pinnace.

Andrew made friends with the three ships' boys
on board. They taught him to chew the ends of hemp
rope to get dizzy and tried to get him to climb the
masts like they did, but his stomach wouldn't take it.
They showed him how to roll dice and play a game
with bright-colored cards they'd got from one of the
sailors. The boys couldn't read, but they were masters
at playing cards.

Andrew was glad to have friends his own age,
though they seemed more like men than boys. They
talked about girls they knew and doing things he had
no idea of. What he missed, home and family, counted

for nothing with them; the *Tyger* was as much home as they knew.

They got Andrew to bet. He won a few times, then he began to lose.

"Pay up!" the biggest one demanded.

Andrew didn't have any money.

"Go double-or-nothing, then."

He lost again.

Now he owed twopence. He was employed by Mr. Harriot and earning a wage, but he was too ashamed to approach him. He went to Tremayne.

"I need twopence," he said.

"For what?"

"To pay the ships' boys."

Slowly, Tremayne got the story.

"They took you!" he said with a grim smile as he handed Andrew the coins. "The old trick—they let you win just enough to make you think you knew what you were doing, then they rigged the game. You got cheated!"

Andrew said nothing. He felt sick. It wasn't the money; it was feeling alone and different. He'd felt close to those boys—the way he'd felt about his friends at school and William. To the ships' boys, though, he was nothing more than a pocket to empty.

They were thirty-two days out from the Canaries

when Salt announced New World land, the island of Puerto Rico. He and the Indians smelled it at the same time. The Indians sang a long single-note chant as the dog barked. The breeze was sweet, full of flowers.

The ship's water was stale, the barrels green and slimy, teeming with worms. Everyone was hungry for fresh fruit and greens, anything but ship biscuit and salt pork.

Following the map Tremayne and Andrew had stolen from the Frenchman, the admiral found an un-inhabited harbor safe from Spanish eyes. The land had been freshly worked, though; there were Spaniards around.

The men were organized into teams, the largest to throw up a wall of pointed logs in case Spaniards at-tacked, another to scour the green mold from the water barrels and refill them, the third to go after cas-sava root to make bread. They found plenty in the worked fields. The bread was sweet and good. Mr. Harriot helped Tremayne and Andrew gather sugar and banana roots to try at Roanoke.

The explorers suffered from sunburn and biting flies until Manteo and Wanchese showed them a root to pulp and rub on their bodies.

Once the palisade was up, Andrew joined the

carpenters building a pinnace to replace the one lost in the storm. This was the work he liked best: the tools and smells of fresh-shaved wood reminded him of helping his father do carpentry work back at Stillwell.

He was proud to show he knew how to manage the drills and planes and measure angles. "If you don't like Virginia, lad, we'll take you on as apprentice," the *Tyger*'s master carpenter announced. That warmed Andrew; it made up for the hurt he'd felt at being cheated by the ships' boys.

In less than a week they'd fashioned a keel and laid the ribs out like fish bones. A week later they launched her. She was green and leaky, but the admiral ordered the fleet to sail.

Andrew stood with Tremayne and Mr. Harriot, watching as the island grew small behind them. "How soon do we make Virginia?" he asked, sure that was where they were headed at last.

"Ah," said Mr. Harriot, his mouth tightening. "The admiral has orders from the investors to take prizes, and even if he didn't, he would."

Sure enough, down came the English flags and up went the Spanish. The admiral turned pirate and went hunting along the sea-lanes. Neither Mr. Harriot nor Tremayne seemed surprised, so Andrew kept his mouth shut. All hours the admiral kept the ships' boys, slight and quick as cats, watching from the mast tops. It made Andrew queasy to look up at them swaying like birds in a storm.

It was early morning. Andrew was wetting the apple shoots with his share of fresh water when he heard the yell—

"Sail! Sail!" One of the gamblers had spotted a merchantman.

There wasn't much wind, and the loaded *Tyger* was heavy and slow. The Spaniard tried to escape. Admiral Grenville ordered up every sail he could hang and formed teams to wet them so they'd hold what wind there was. Andrew was perched ten feet above deck, cheering and yelling in time with the others as he passed up the heavy buckets and lowered the empties.

Admiral Grenville was the better sailor. By midafternoon the *Tyger* had drawn close, firing shots from her one small swivel cannon and shooting flaming arrows to set the Spaniards' rigging afire.

The Spaniards shot back as good as they got and more. Andrew dodged fire arrows as he raced with buckets of seawater to douse flames. Slowly they pulled alongside, splinters flying as the *Tyger*'s sailors threw anchors and grappling irons to haul in the enemy. The boy leapt to join the haulers on the thick rope just as the sailor next to him went down with a scream, blood jetting from his neck; another held his arm, half off at the shoulder. Andrew pulled with everything he had; he pulled for three.

As the two ships bumped together, scraping and grinding, the *Tyger*'s sailors, explorers, and Indians jumped across to the Spaniard, yelling like madmen and screaming an eerie high-pitched Indian war whoop. Andrew screamed too, as loud as he could, as he held on to his haul line.

He'd grown up on stories that the English are the bloodthirstiest soldiers in the world, thinking first about honor and last about safety as each goes after his own prize. That afternoon, he learned it was the same with the Indians. As for the Spanish, he discovered they could be fierce fighters too, but they were practical. When the Spanish captain realized what he faced, he allowed capture and got good treatment. Andrew couldn't imagine Admiral Grenville giving up like that.

The boy watched as Manteo and Wanchese draped themselves in plundered calico and paraded, singing and chanting their high strange music, on the *Tyger*'s deck. Others piled up what they could use of the Spaniards' cargo—barrels of wine, crates of cloth, coops of chickens.

Mr. Harriot and Tremayne came and stood beside him while folks on deck figured their gains. "The ship is new," Mr. Harriot said. "She'll bring plenty back home in England! And those fancy prisoners—they'll bring good ransoms! The Queen and Sir Walter will do well, the investors too. And us, we'll get shares!"

"Me?" asked Andrew. "I'll get a share too?"

"Indeed you will, same prize money as Tremayne and me," Mr. Harriot said with a big smile. A shiver of pride went over the boy. His father could use the money.

They sailed along the Florida channel and up the Virginia coast, stitching past its line of sheltering islands. The pilot said the one they sought lay inside the outer ones. Suddenly Andrew felt the ship turn.

The heavily laden *Tyger* rode deep. She needed fifteen feet depth of water for clear sailing.

Roanoke Island was mostly flat and low, twenty miles long, six across at the widest. On the map it was shaped like one of Pena's Spanish roots, the plant he called potato. As they approached it, Andrew and one of the ships' boys were sent to perch far forward on the bowsprit to measure the depth of water. Their weighted lines were marked every half foot. They took turns calling out their soundings to the admiral. It was as they'd been warned: shallows all around.

It was late afternoon. The admiral was wary. Although they were well off from the island, the ship was already in shallows. The sounders were calling, "Twenty-one!" "Twenty!" then "Eighteen!" when Admiral Grenville ordered, "Drop sail! Drop anchor!"

As the anchors rumbled out on their chains, a cloud of white cranes rose from the marsh with a cry like an army of men shouting all together. To Andrew, it was a greeting. It thrilled him like hearing that deep organ chord at St. Paul's Cathedral a year before.

Tremayne came and stood beside him. The long line of sunset was bright gold shading up to crimson. The breeze carried a sweet scent of tidewater and sun-warmed marsh. The man who had been his teacher smiled and shook his head. "Do you remember when I saw you off to London, I asked you to bring me news? You did better! You brought me to the news!"

29

SHIPWRECK!

At dusk, from the *Tyger*'s deck, they saw Indians on-shore. Admiral Grenville made signs of greeting, but the Indians ran away. That night, on board, they heard a harsh, wavering conch horn signal that carried for miles. "They send news of us," Manteo explained.

The gentlemen unpacked their finery to dress for the landing.

They attempted it early the next morning. Waves and eddies roiled the channel as the *Tyger* poked its way. The chart the first exploring captains had made was useless. Storms and drifting sand had changed the inlets.

Andrew clung to the bowsprit like a spider, legs around, one hand holding as he sounded the channel depths with the other. The vessel pitched and heaved with the rolls of water and the pushing wind.

"Sixteen!" the boy behind him yelled, calling the number from his marked rope.

Andrew's showed less than twelve.

"Eleven!" he hollered as a huge roller hurled the ship forward.

The cord in his hand went slack as the *Tyger* ran aground with a crash like falling timber. It was all Andrew could do to hang on to the narrow spar as he spun like a toy on a stick. Then another wave sent the ship rolling far to port and he was pitched into the churning water along with crates and chunks of broken wood. As he fell in, one of the heavy crates tore his ear and banged his shoulder.

Roller after roller smacked the *Tyger*, each one breaking more of her bones. There were yells and screams as rigging snapped like kindling. Gagging on seawater, the boy splashed frantically and fought for breath. His left arm hurt. His boots were pulling him down. Then Pena's voice came to him: "On your back. Rest. Then make like the frog."

He rolled over on his back. It was hard to kick with his boots on. Slowly, he worked them off. Then he rested, panting and vomiting. At last he made like a frog for land.

Salt! Where was Salt?

The wind shifted and the ship broke free. The

admiral brought her, half sunk, to anchor some distance from the island.

Two deckhands and the ships' boy who'd spotted the prize a few days before were missing.

That afternoon, the sailors began ferrying the explorers to shore in the small boats. Andrew heard there were many injured. He went out to the *Tyger* to help Tremayne and Mr. Harriot as they worked with the ship's surgeon.

They were sent to a sailor whose leg bone was sticking out like a piece of snapped wood. Andrew had watched his mother set such breaks. Tremayne gave the sailor a drink of spirits, then tied him down. The sailor's groans became howls as the boy used all his strength to force the ends of bone together and then probed the wound to fish out splinters.

That done, he rinsed the swollen purple mess with strong wine and braced it with splints tied tight around with cords.

Next was a man with his scalp torn open. Blood gushed when they lifted his bandage. Andrew sewed him up the way you'd stitch shut a sack, loop over and thread under.

Tremayne then stitched Andrew's torn ear. He'd had no practice at this work; his stitching hurt more than the crate's tearing. He fixed the tear, but he didn't line it up properly.

The sailors, meanwhile, ferried to shore what could be saved of the expedition's food. There wasn't much. The *Tyger*'s hold was deep in brine. The barrels of flour were soaked, the dried meat and stockfish all spoiled.

A gentleman fussed about damage to his yellow silk suit.

They were one hundred four explorers. With what they'd saved and counting the supplies not needed on the other ships, they had food for twenty days. The *Tyger* had carried most of their stores because the admiral feared the crews' stealing. The best of what they had left was cheese. Andrew had never liked cheese.

Right then he didn't think about their difficulties. The place was beautiful, unlike any he'd ever seen, flat and noisy in constant sea wind, slap of water, rustling reed meadows along the shore, thick green brush a little ways inland, then immense oaks bearded with silver moss. Cypress grew tall out of the water; there were groves of great spiked cedar trees. The soil was black and sandy. He scooped up a handful and made a ball. It held. He sniffed it and tasted it. *I can grow anything in this,* he thought. Near the fort, there were trees blooming white blossoms large as saucers. A gray and white bird mocked his whistle; when it flew, it looked like a wheel turning.

Exhausted and half sick from salt water as he was, Andrew had never felt happier in his life. A glow of pride and relief warmed him. "I made it," he said to himself. "I made it to America!"

Manteo and Wanchese showed the explorers how

to cut fragrant cedar boughs for their beds. As Andrew and Tremayne worked, the wind and swamp smells filled their heads. There were whitecaps on the gray-brown water. The water glinted like silver from the silt in it. Strange birds sang. Some were red, some blue with touches of black. In the warm sunlight, the air was heavy with green and growing.

In the last light, Tremayne helped Andrew dig slits to heel in the apple shoots until they could plant them proper. "Water them good!" the boy heard Pena saying. There was no fresh water close by. Anyway, he didn't have a bucket. "Tomorrow!" he whispered, touching the closest one.

When he came into the fort, one of the explorers brought a candle to look at his swollen ear.

"I saw it happen," the man said. "It was a crate of chickens did it. I was sure you'd sink when it crowned you." He bathed the injured ear with the stinging spirits they called aqua vitae, or "water of life."

The next day, the man whose scalp Andrew had stitched found Salt on the island, weak and unsteady, sick from swallowing seawater.

That afternoon a small party of warriors came up, armed but curious. They'd seen white men before. They recognized Manteo and Wanchese.

Manteo repeated in Algonquin what the explorers' land captain, Captain Lane, told him to say:

"Make ready! Our chief will soon present himself to your chief. He brings word from the ruler of these lands, Sir Walter Raleigh, and from Big Chief Elizabeth, the chief of all chiefs."

Andrew stood beside Mr. Harriot as Manteo spoke in case there was interpreting to do. There wasn't. The warriors looked hard at Manteo, then left without speaking.

Sir Walter would have begun friendlier, Andrew thought. *Captain Lane makes us sound like Spaniards.*

30

TO CHIEF PEMISAPAN

On hearing his warriors' report that the English chief was going to visit, Chief Pemisapan called all his lesser chiefs to his lodge. He ruled the island and the mainland opposite. The mile of water that separated them was so shallow a man could walk most of the way when the tide was out.

The next morning, Captain Lane ordered Wanchese and Manteo to take him across to Pemisapan. Mr. Harriot, Tremayne, and Andrew were to go along. Sir Walter had given the captain written instructions that Mr. Harriot was to accompany every mission, with Tremayne as his assistant and Andrew as secretary to write the daily log and help interpret.

By now Manteo had learned enough English to get along, and Mr. Harriot and Andrew knew basic Algonquin.

"I don't expect trouble," Captain Lane announced, "but to impress them we'll go with a squad of soldiers in armor. We'll be asking for food. We'll want those people to be in a willing mood."

That wasn't the way they'd planned their first meeting with the natives when they'd sat with Sir Walter in the turret back at Durham House. It was as if the shipwreck and loss of food had changed everything. Captain Lane was preparing for war. He was acting like a Spaniard!

Andrew looked at Mr. Harriot. The tall man's lips were pressed tight together.

Mr. Harriot spoke with Manteo for a moment.

"Manteo suggests no weapons and we take the chief a gift," he said.

The captain glared. "You may trust them; I do not. We travel as soldiers," he exclaimed. "My men and I will wear armor and carry weapons. As for gifts, I have a small knife and some trinkets in this bag."

"More, for when you ask for the food," Manteo whispered to Mr. Harriot. "That!" he said, pointing to a large copper pot.

"Manteo suggests we take that as well," said Mr. Harriot.

"You'll spoil them from the start," the captain

muttered, "but if that's what you want to do, you can have Andrew lug it."

Approaching Pemisapan's village, the Englishmen clanked past rough-kept fields of corn with beans and yellow-blooming squash underneath. Nearby there were smaller plots of tobacco.

"How much crop do they save?" Mr. Harriot asked.

"Enough to eat through winter and plant in spring," Manteo replied, "unless the cold lasts long or the seeds rot."

The Indians' dogs set up a racket. Salt growled. Andrew picked him up. He didn't fit in the boy's pocket anymore.

A fence of sharpened poles dug in and laced together with vine ropes surrounded a cluster of lodges made of cedar hoops covered with reed mats.

One lodge stood apart. There were paths to the others, no path to that one.

"Who lives there?" Andrew asked.

"Our dead chiefs and priests," Manteo replied. "You put yours in the ground; we keep ours."

The boy looked puzzled.

"When they die, we take out the guts," Manteo explained. "We lay their bodies on a shelf with medicine root to eat in the next world. When the flesh rots away, we wrap their bones in what's left of their skins."

Andrew wanted to know what the medicine root was, but just then Captain Lane marched up. "Tidy!" he announced with a sweep of his hands. "A good camp, well protected."

The Indians stood silent, watching the English soldiers approach, noisy and awkward, red-faced and sweating as sunlight glinted off their polished armor.

Andrew felt someone staring at him. He turned and saw a broad-faced Indian boy his age standing apart. He looked like a younger Manteo. Manteo noticed him too and waved him over.

"My brother's son," he explained as the boy approached, his eyes fixed on Andrew. Manteo talked with him for a moment in a low voice that Andrew could not make out.

"His name is Sky. He came when he saw your ships passing," Manteo explained. "His village is called Ocracoke, an island to the south. He says your spirit called him. His father is a healer, a kind of priest; his grandfather too. He will be the same."

"My spirit called him?" Andrew asked.

"Yes," said Manteo. "He says it spoke when he saw the ships. He set out at once. He just got here."

The back of Andrew's neck prickled as the Indian

boy searched his face, hands, and feet. What was he looking for? His eyes were black, unblinking. They gave no sign; it was as if he were studying a rock. He was fine-looking, shorter and thicker than Andrew. He wore a plain deerskin apron around his waist and a drilled claw the size of a little finger from a leather strip at his neck. His silky black hair was cropped short.

As Tremayne and Mr. Harriot moved on, Sky walked close beside Andrew.

Tremayne pointed to the chiefs' guards. Their heads were shaved bare save for a long lock on the left side, oiled and combed. Their fingernails were long as claws.

"Look at their scars!" Tremayne whispered.

So far as Andrew knew, Manteo's body and Wanchese's were unmarked. The older men he saw now had marks burned into their backs and upper arms: a long arrow on one, an "X" on another, four arrows diminishing in length on a third, three uniform arrows on a fourth.

"What are the marks for?" he asked.

"Allegiance marks," Manteo explained. "You carry a flag for your Queen; our most powerful warriors carry a mark. Your men can switch sides," he said with a smile. "Ours cannot, unless they are captured and made slaves. Wanchese is marked. On the inside of his leg—here," he said, pointing to his upper thigh. "Here he carries a mark."

The Englishmen had not known Wanchese was allied to one of the chiefs.

"Are you marked?" Andrew asked.

"No," Manteo replied. "I am not a warrior. When I left here, I was studying to be a priest."

Pemisapan met them with his council. He said nothing. His head was shaved bare, save for a lock on one side tied in an oiled knot stuck with feathers and a shrunken hand. His teeth were small and wide-spaced. On his chest he wore a plate of beaten copper the shape and size of a man's palm. Its gleam caught the captain's eye.

Wanchese introduced Captain Lane to the assembly in the Indian language. The captain stood tall, holding the silver-headed pole of polished wood, called a mace, that signified his office. In his other hand he held the leather sack of presents.

Captain Lane did not know Algonquin, so he spoke his English extra loud.

"I represent the owner of this land, Sir Walter Raleigh, Lord of Virginia!"

He thumped the pole.

"We are all the Queen's subjects! She is the chief of all chiefs."

Two more thumps.

"We are here to introduce you to the Reformed Christian religion!"

Several thumps.

The Indians stood motionless, their eyes on the leather sack.

The captain looked to his soldiers to clap. He then presented a small knife to Chief Pemisapan. The captain had bronze bells and tin whistles for the others.

The captain ordered his men to rattle the bells and blow on the whistles as they passed them out. The Indians did nothing with them. They were not pleased;

knives would have suited them better. They cut with sharpened oyster shells and chipped stones.

The captain motioned to Mr. Harriot. "Now!" he said in a low voice.

Mr. Harriot had been ordered to show the Indians something of his science. As Andrew gathered up twigs and dry leaves, Mr. Harriot took a magnifying glass from his pocket and passed it among the chiefs.

"It will make fire," he told them in Algonquin.

Their looks revealed nothing.

He positioned the lens to beam the sun against Andrew's pile of tinder. In a moment a curl of smoke rose, then a lick of flame.

The lesser chiefs whispered among themselves.

"They say your power to call fire means you are a priest," Manteo explained. "They say that is why you do not dress like the others."

Andrew caught Sky's eye as he watched. "I will show you," he whispered in the boy's language. Sky nodded and smiled a little.

A feast was offered. While the women put out food, Andrew went to Mr. Harriot.

"May I give him a present?" he asked, pointing to Sky. "He is Manteo's nephew."

Mr. Harriot fumbled in his deep pocket.

"I have more of the captain's trinkets for the chiefs—bells and whistles—but it won't do to give him any of those.

"How about this?" he asked, pulling out a chipped piece of lens glass.

Andrew took it.

"A gift," he said as he held it out to Sky. "A piece of the fire stone."

Sky nodded as he studied it carefully, feeling the edge. Suddenly he turned and ran back to the lodges. He returned with a claw like the one he wore.

"My gift," he said. "Your spirit told me to bring

it. Bear claw," he added. "I'll bore it so you can wear it like mine. It will protect you."

The smell of food cooking made them hungry. They went to where the chief's allegiance men were signaling the English to sit.

The feast was a stew of corn and beans together with broiled meat cooked on wooden spits. Later, the squaws baked corn cakes on the heated rocks. Sky sat with Manteo and Andrew. As soon as the women served the corn cakes, the Indian boy tossed a fistful of dried corn on the hot rocks. Andrew started when the first grains popped. Sky laughed at his surprise. He grabbed up the white puffs and ate them. Then he handed a fistful of the popped corn to Andrew.

As the biggest of the marked guards pulled his meat from a spit, he pointed to Salt and gestured as if to skewer and cook him in the same way. The Indians and the English laughed together as Andrew gathered the dog in his arms. Sky did not laugh.

There was no beer, wine, or any spirit. The Indians' drink was water flavored with sassafras root. It was not sweet; nothing the Indians ate or drank was sweet.

"The grapes we see," Mr. Harriot asked Manteo. "What do you make with them?"

Manteo shook his head. He puckered his mouth to show their sourness.

"Do you make wine?"

He shook his head.

"Do you brew with corn?"

Again he shook his head. "You want beer," Manteo said. "We don't make beer. To get like you with much beer, we smoke tobacco and dance!"

After dinner the warriors gathered in a circle around the fire pit, clapping to a rhythm of drums, rattles, and a sort of flute as they sang in high voices. Suddenly a small band of black-painted priests appeared wearing antlers on their heads. They formed a smaller circle inside the larger. They shook their heads and waved green boughs up and down as they danced in the opposite direction, singing their own music. Then, as if on signal, the rattles and the singing stilled.

Chief Pemisapan looked at Captain Lane and spoke slowly in a deep gravelly voice.

The captain looked at Mr. Harriot. "What does he want?" he whispered.

"Your speech of thanks."

"You make it," said the captain. "And order food for the others."

"Send for the big pot," Mr. Harriot commanded as he stepped forward and spoke in the Indians' tongue.

"We have enjoyed your feast," he said slowly, bowing with his hands pressed together. "The hundred back at the fort would like the same for a week. In thanks, we will make Chief Pemisapan gift of a fine copper pot."

The chief and his council sat silent as they waited for the captain's party to bring the pot.

Mr. Harriot pointed to show they should place it at the chief's feet.

After a long pause, Pemisapan nodded slowly.

It was late afternoon when the explorers rowed back across the channel to the fort.

"Perhaps we feed on copper pots this winter," the captain said. "We have plenty; the *Tyger*'s wetting didn't spoil them!"

He had learned the Indian word for the piece of bright metal the chief wore on his chest. He had smiled broadly at Pemisapan all through the feast and pointed to show that he wanted to hold it, but the chief wouldn't take it off.

"Wassador!" the captain announced as they paddled. "We must find where they mine it!

"Mr. Harriot," he called in a loud voice. "That name the Indians call us by—'Mucksoquick' or some such—is that their word for God?"

Mr. Harriot pursed his lips. "It means, sir, 'They wear fine clothes.'"

The man who laughed caught the heavy end of the captain's mace.

"Their name for him is 'Big Thumps-a-Stick,'" Mr. Harriot whispered to Tremayne.

When they landed, Tremayne and Andrew walked with Mr. Harriot up to the fort.

"Manteo says game and fish grow scarce here in winter," Mr. Harriot said. "We came as owners; we find ourselves guests. It will take all our science to stay fed. Our need for grain will soon outstrip theirs for copper pots."

Salt was trotting beside Andrew. Suddenly he shot into the brush. He came back with a red squirrel.

"His science will feed him well enough," said Tremayne with a laugh.

As Andrew reached to look at it, Salt snarled. He wagged his tail, but he would not let go. He ate it on the spot.

That afternoon, an Indian found in the fish traps a blue velvet jacket trimmed with silver lace. For days almost every tide brought in other English goods. Andrew was startled to encounter a warrior sitting on the shore in a long London coat with gold buttons. He was holding a book.

31

WASSADOR

The next morning, Andrew and Tremayne rowed out to the *Tyger* to see their patients. The broken leg they'd set was hot and inflamed, dark with a crust of dried pus where the bone had come out. They dosed the sailor with spirits and scraped the wound open to drain it.

"Skip all that!" the sailor growled as Andrew dug in his saddlebag for the herb his mother used for open wounds. "Wash it with salt water. That heals better than your blasted leaves!"

They dipped up bucketfuls of cold seawater and poured them over.

Mr. Harriot met them when they got back to the fort.

"The captain says we must go to Chief Pemisapan

to learn about their mines of metal. We'll row across after dinner."

Andrew picked up his long package of hobby-horses and filled a saddlebag with toys for the bright-eyed children he'd seen.

As they paddled across the channel, Mr. Harriot asked Wanchese if he knew of any mines around.

"No."

"Any deep pits your people visit?"

"There is a cave on the mainland," Wanchese replied. "It is a sacred place."

"Is there metal in it?" Mr. Harriot asked.

"I've never been there. Only the priests go."

"Is it far?"

"It is where the mountains begin. The priests go with no food. They chew a root. They are gone for days."

"Is that the root your priests lay beside the dead priests and chiefs?" Andrew asked.

Wanchese shrugged. "I don't know. I am not a priest."

Mr. Harriot met Chief Pemisapan in his lodge.

"We have come to find the wassador," he said. "Where does it come from?"

"A great distance," the chief said.

"Does it come from the priests' cave?" Mr. Harriot asked.

Pemisapan turned away. His guards motioned the visitors out.

As they walked back to the boats, Andrew handed out tops and toy animals to the children, who appeared like magic as soon as he opened his saddlebag. Their high chirping voices filled the air like music. Then he unwrapped the hobbyhorses.

The children went silent, staring. Andrew took one and pretended to ride it around the fire pit. The children didn't move.

Sky had come up to watch. "Deer," he called in Algonquin as he took one and galloped. "The English brings us deer."

Slowly, one of the girls came forward and took one. She didn't ride it, though; she carried it to her lodge. Others did the same.

"Manteo," Andrew called. "May I bring Sky to the fort?"

Manteo looked at Mr. Harriot. The tall man nodded.

In the boat, Sky showed Andrew his bear claw gift, now bored and strung on a cord like his. "You'll wear it?" he asked, pointing that Andrew should bend his head. Sky hung the claw around his neck. "Us," he said, pointing first to himself, then at Andrew. "We."

Mr. Harriot reported to Captain Lane on his useless meeting with Pemisapan.

"He's hiding it!" the captain muttered. "The priests' cave must be where it comes from. As soon as we have the fort in good order, we'll go there."

He noticed the claw around Andrew's neck. He leaned forward, peering. "What heathenish thing are you wearing, boy?"

Andrew touched the claw. "A gift, sir, from one who studies their medicine," he said in a strong voice.

"Some gift! Some medicine!" the captain harrumphed.

"It's proof that we're making friends here," Mr. Harriot said quietly.

"Don't get too friendly with them," the captain grumbled. "Remember, they're savages!"

Late that afternoon, while Captain Lane was clambering around the base of the fort checking foundations, a copperhead struck him deep in the calf just above his boot top. He fell hard, thrashing and bellowing.

Andrew came running. He'd heard about the copper-headed snakes.

"Their bite is deadly," the exploring captains had reported. "We lost a man to snakebite—his face blotched purple as he died in agony."

While Mr. Harriot and Tremayne fashioned a tourniquet to keep the poison from traveling up the captain's body to his heart, Andrew went for Sky. "The captain!" he yelled. "A snake! You must save him! Please!" Together they rushed to where the captain writhed and groaned.

The Indian boy got close and looked at the wound, then he grabbed Andrew's hand and ran for the woods. "White root!" he yelled. "We go for white root!" He found the plant, ripped it up, and raced back.

Andrew translated for him. "You two," Sky ordered, pointing to Tremayne and Mr. Harriot, "sit on the captain's back to keep him still for me to do my work."

While the two men struggled to control the frantic captain, the Indian boy shut his eyes for an instant, chanted rapidly in a high singsong voice, then took a sharp-edged oyster shell from the pouch at his waist. He slashed a deep "X" over the bite with more force than Andrew imagined he had. Then he squeezed the wound hard to make it bleed and sucked it. He spat out the poisoned blood, sucked again and spat again, then chewed the white root and spat his chaw into the wound. He pointed that Andrew should tie a cloth to hold the medicine in place.

The captain's leg turned black. The "X" Sky cut left a white scar, and where the tourniquet had cut into the captain's thigh he was sore for months, but he recovered. The upshot was he never objected to Sky's staying in the fort.

In the logbook he kept for Mr. Harriot, Andrew wrote down Sky's description of the snakeroot and other medicine plants his friend pointed out.

"But the plant, the root—we use it with the prayer," Sky explained. "That's what gives it power. Each illness, each remedy, has its prayer."

"Was that what you cried out before you cut Captain Lane?"

"Yes."

"Can you teach me?" Andrew asked.

"Only the shaman—the chief priest," Sky replied. "I am not allowed."

Andrew wondered what Sir Walter would make of the idea that the shaman's prayers gave power to their medicines.

Sky followed Mr. Harriot close as a shadow when he wasn't with Andrew. He asked so many questions the tall man took to calling him Why. He was curious about everything—how magnets worked, why the English cleaned their teeth, what money was, why letters had sounds.

Of all the new strange things he saw, Sky asked for only one: a bright steel sewing needle from Mr. Harriot's kit. He carefully worked it into the rawhide strip around his neck just above the bear claw so it gleamed like a bit of stitching.

He showed Andrew how to find nests to raid for eggs they ate raw on the spot, the juice of the plant to smear on himself for stings, and how to chew spruce gum to get a sweet taste in the mouth. They experimented making fires with the lenses. One afternoon, as they raced to see who could get a blaze going first, the wind picked up suddenly and sent their flames roaring toward the fort. They admitted nothing as they helped the men cut brush and clear a swath to contain the fire, but Andrew could tell Mr. Harriot knew.

Andrew and Sky drew pictures for each other to teach their words. Sky picked up English as fast as Andrew added to his Algonquin.

They built a secret perch of limbs fastened with treenails high in an oak tree hung with grapevines. The only way to it was up the vines. No one could see them, but they could see the fort and across the sound. One afternoon, to surprise his friend, Andrew carried up

Mr. Harriot's glass for looking at a distance. The Indian boy's mouth fell open when he put the tube to his eye. He held his breath as he lowered it, looked out across the sound, then raised it again. "Oooh!" he exclaimed. "A priest's eye!"

They made a game of swinging out on the vines over the red clay gully below—each daring the other to push off harder and swing higher, until Andrew crashed when the vine he swung on broke. He lay like dead until Sky revived him with the juice of skunkweed.

One hot, idle afternoon, Andrew asked Sky, "Do you do acting with masks?"

"The priests do," said Sky, "to call for rain and healing and victory over our enemies. We have medicine masks, masks for war, masks for dancing."

"Do you put on plays with them to entertain the people?"

"Sometimes, to show how stupid our enemies are and give courage to our warriors."

"My favorite story is about a boy named Galahad," said Andrew. "There's a test. He does something no one else can do."

"How?" Sky asked. "Was he the bravest?"

"No. He had the truest heart."

Sky nodded. "Our warriors and apprentice priests

face such a test going into manhood. I will face such a test." He paused. He would not say more.

"Shall we make masks and act the story for the company?" Andrew asked.

"Yes."

They spent days working out their parts and making the masks. Sky played Galahad. The explorers all knew the story and applauded. Mr. Harriot proposed they do it for the children in Pemisapan's village.

"No," said Sky. "It's too much like the trial our young men go through. They will think we mock them."

At last Captain Lane was ready to go to the priests' cave. With supplies for a week and tools to gather samples of rock, the survey team paddled across the channel. Salt and Sky rode with Andrew in Tremayne's boat.

Again Mr. Harriot asked Pemisapan about the cave.

"You cannot go there," the chief said in his slow deep voice. "Only the priests."

"We go as priests," said Mr. Harriot quietly. "Summon yours. I will show you once more I am one of them."

A priest of science, Andrew thought. *A priest like Doctor Dee. Not a church priest.*

When the chief's priests came, Mr. Harriot took a packet of iron filings from his pocket and emptied it on the ground. As he waved his magnetized blade over the pieces of metal, he drew them up.

He then pulled out his compass and showed its blue needle pointing north. With his blade he made it point to him. As he backed away, it aimed north again.

The Indians stared like stones and said nothing.

Mr. Harriot put more iron filings on the ground and held out the compass to Chief Pemisapan. "Let your priests raise the grains and move the needle," he said.

No one moved.

After a long silence, Pemisapan nodded. He motioned to two of his allegiance men. "Lead them to the priests' cave," he ordered.

As the company set out, Sky walked beside Andrew. One of the allegiance men stopped and ordered the Indian boy back.

"No," said Manteo. "He is of my tribe, not yours. He goes with me."

They marched all that day and much of the next. The land was smooth as it sloped upward through groves of trees and open meadows.

"This land will make wonderful farms," Andrew told Mr. Harriot as he wrote in the journal that night.

"What do you mean?"

"It is smooth, there are no rocks, the loamy soil."

Mr. Harriot looked up. "The soil?" he asked. "What's special about the soil?"

"The black in it," Andrew explained. "And its sweetness. The color shows its richness. I dug where we stopped for dinner—the black goes down more than a foot. The thick grasses show there's limestone underneath. That makes it sweet.

"It's like the long slope from Exeter down to Plymouth," the boy continued. "It would take nothing to run cattle here. Pigs would grow fat in the woods."

Mr. Harriot was a city man. Andrew was a farmer's son. He showed Mr. Harriot Virginia through a farmer's eyes.

The following day, Captain Lane was in good spirits as they approached the steep hills where the cave was.

"This is what we came for!" he exclaimed. "Gold!"

The path was well-worn, then rougher and rougher over broken stone. At last the allegiance men pointed out the cave's opening between cracks of an overhanging ledge. Then they turned and left.

"What will we burn for light?" the captain asked.

Manteo pointed to a tall pine. "The hard pitch wood at the center burns long."

The day was overcast. The burning glass wouldn't work, so Manteo made fire the Indian way, twisting a dry stick into the slack cord of a short bow, then pushing one end of the stick into a shallow hole in a bit of dry wood with shavings piled around. As he sawed the bow back and forth, the stick spun and the rubbing end got hot. Soon the stuff around it was on fire.

They crawled into the cave on their bellies. It was dark and close. Andrew fought back his sick feeling about being in tight places. The farther in they went, the darker it got. Then there was a turn and the last daylight was gone! He forced himself to keep up.

The cave went deep, shafts dividing off like tree branches. The way was low and narrow. At every turning, Manteo kept to the left. They stooped and crawled. At some turnings the flares burned brighter and they breathed fresher air. It was damp. They stopped often to chip off pieces of rock.

Suddenly the tunnel opened out to where a man could almost stand. Cool air poured in, the torches flared. There were drawings of hunters, animals, and strange shapes like large insects scratched in the stone. The hunters carried spears and bows. The insects, large as men, held drums, rattles, and reed pipes. In the torches' flickerings, the shapes glowed white and seemed to move, the hunters lunging toward their prey as the insect musicians played and danced.

They heard what sounded like organ music. Andrew looked at Sky. He gave a quick nod.

Mr. Harriot signaled that he heard it too. "The wind," he said.

Manteo stared at the images like one in prayer. "The drawings are from long ago," he said finally. "This big one is our god Okeus." He pointed.

It was a large-headed figure with huge eyes and the features of man and woman. It looked like the idol he and Wanchese had prayed to on board the ship.

In front of the drawings there was a large earthenware dish filled with bones, seashells, and a few small pieces of copper bearing the image of Okeus.

Captain Lane kicked over the dish and picked out the pieces of copper.

"No!" Manteo exclaimed. "Those things were given to the god!"

"You do not give me orders!" the captain snarled as he pocketed the medals.

Andrew was ashamed. From what he'd heard, that was the way Spaniards behaved.

On the return, they kept to the right. By the time

they should have reached the entrance, their torches were almost spent. Somewhere they'd missed a turn. They were lost! Andrew's stomach twisted.

The captain swore as he grabbed one of the torches and started back. It was just a few paces to where the cave divided and then divided again. He stopped. "Which way did we come?" he yelled. No one answered.

Andrew was panting. This was worse than being in the well.

"Ask him," Sky whispered, pointing to the dog.

"Back, Salt!" Andrew ordered. "Go back!"

Sniffing carefully, the dog led them. Then the last torch guttered out, and they found themselves in utter darkness. It felt like being buried alive in crow feathers.

Andrew reached for the dog's tail. "Take hands," he called.

Sky took his.

"Go, Salt!"

At last, after what seemed like hours of crawling and sweating, they saw daylight. The dry fresh air was the sweetest Andrew had ever breathed.

At the cave mouth, Mr. Harriot sorted the chips of rock he'd taken.

"Is there gold?" the captain asked.

"Limestone," Mr. Harriot said, pointing to one pile. "Good for mortar. And here, rag—good building stone. And this one, iron."

"Is there ore?" the captain asked again, louder.

"Iron, yes," said Mr. Harriot, looking up at him without expression. "Gold, no."

32

FROM THE FORT

24 August, 1585

Dear Family and Rebecca,

The Tyger sails for England tomorrow. I set the leg of the sailor who brings this. He does not limp! He will tell you how it is with us. I am well. We've had little illness, and none of the company has died. Food is short, though; no one grows fat.

I think Virginia could feed all England. Without plow or manure, the Indian women get good crops. When a field wears out, the men clear forest to make new.

We want to buy a worn-out field to experiment, but no one understands what we mean by "buying." Manteo, our Indian friend, says no one owns land.

He says you can only own a thing you can carry, like the earring he got from the Queen.

Mornings, I work as apprentice to the carpenters. The men say Father taught me well. We build boats and wagons and improve the fort. Parts of it wash away in every gale. Our captain says Virginia storms do us worse than Spanish cannon ever could. The Indians do not know wheels. Men drag their loads on long poles.

I go everywhere with Mr. Harriot. At night I write the day's journal as he directs. I tend the apples and the English seeds we planted. The apples have taken and most of the seeds thrive too, but we arrived too late to get any crop.

No one is idle. We muster to trumpet calls at dawn and drill to fight Spaniards and natives. To Captain Lane, both are enemy and we are troops. So far he's kept us safe and in order with promise of the lash and worse for those who would disobey. "Idle hands are the devil's playthings" is his rule. Sir Walter would deal kinder with the Indians, I think.

An Indian boy my age teaches me medicine plants and how to track, trap, and weave with grass. I am learning the Algonquin tongue. They have no writing. When a snake struck the captain, Sky saved him with a root.

Some of the chiefs wear pearls. This small one is for Rebecca. Manteo found it in an oyster. The Indians weave the cloth it comes in from silk grass colored with the juice of a blood-colored root the Indians call puccoon. We've found no pearls in all the oysters we've opened. I am sick of oysters. We eat them roasted, raw, and boiled as we have no fat for frying. The best fat here is bear's, sweeter than any English butter. To bite into a bad oyster is awful. We have opened and eaten so many, our paths in the fort are paved with oyster shells.

I miss you very much, and the dogs. The Indians have dogs, but they are not pets. Sometimes they eat them.

Andrew

33

MR. HARRIOT IS SICK

Virginia's fall color was brighter than England's—vivid oranges, yellows, reds, and purples. The autumn rain was soft and fragrant. In the damp, the fallen leaves made a sweet smell like malting ale. Flights of white geese came over and rested on the marsh, raucousing day and night. For a week the explorers and Indians fattened on roast goose.

It got dark earlier and the sun rose later now. Some mornings there was frost. The men wore wool caps to bed. Andrew slept in his cap for America.

He was spending all his free time with Sky now. The boys spoke English and Algonquin together, each teaching the other. Andrew's world was as strange to Sky as Sky's was to Andrew. Andrew had come to feel closer to Sky than he had to his best friend at school, because each protected the other.

Mr. Harriot's illness began with a cough and sore throat, then turned to a raging fever as he choked on his phlegm.

Captain Lane advised bleeding. He avoided the patient.

Andrew's stomach heaved when Tremayne cut a vein in Mr. Harriot's wrist to release a cup of hot blood. The boy gave him purges to empty his bowels. The patient turned gray. By the hour he wasted away as they watched.

"He's dying," Andrew said, choking back tears. "We need help." He clenched his fists and said a private prayer.

Tremayne asked Manteo and Sky what to do. That afternoon, the two Indians rowed over to the mainland. They returned after supper, saying Mr. Harriot should go to the priests.

He was now delirious.

"Shall we take you to the Indians?" Tremayne asked.

Mr. Harriot's eyelids fluttered. He made no sound. Then his lips formed what looked like "Yes."

Tremayne went to the captain. "Sir, he wishes to go to the Indians."

"Madness!" Captain Lane exclaimed. "Bleed him again! Purge him! Sweat him! In all events, keep him from the savages! In his weakness he'll reveal our secrets."

"What secrets?" Tremayne wondered aloud. "That we're hungry? Who doesn't know that?"

The captain was readying a group to hunt on the mainland. They would be gone for days. Manteo and Wanchese were to lead as scouts.

Manteo couldn't be found when the hunting party gathered at the boats, so they left without him. When the hunters were well across the channel, he appeared.

As Andrew and Tremayne gently rolled Mr. Harriot onto a litter, the tall man groaned. They carried him to the shore. He was surprisingly light. Manteo had a boat the Indians had made by hollowing out a large log with fire and scraping. Sky stood in the water to push them off, then vaulted himself in.

They paddled to a small village Andrew had never seen. The priests were gathered around their sacred fire pit. The one who led them wore a short cloak of bright blue feathers sewed thick together. He gave Manteo a look and nodded at Andrew.

Andrew whispered to Manteo, "What is his name?"

"'He Who Sees Beyond,'" he replied. "He is my brother—Sky's father."

The priests wore scraps of decorated hide and

pouches of colored leather at the waist. Their faces were painted with a paste of red sumac and the blood-colored root, their chests and thighs daubed with yellow clay and dots of blue. One wore the wings of a bird over his ear; another had wrapped his head with a band of snake and weasel skins woven together and crowned with feathers.

Mr. Harriot was unconscious. The priests pointed to show that his litter should be placed close to the fire.

They motioned Tremayne and Andrew back as they closed in around the litter, swaying together and chanting over the body. He Who Sees Beyond waved a clutch of feathers and a writhing copper-headed snake. His deputy shook a carved stick topped with a small white skull. Sky joined the apprentices as they beat drums and shook rattles.

As the chanting and dancing picked up, He Who Sees Beyond sprinkled water on Mr. Harriot. Then he laid flowers on him. The others did the same, until the Englishman's body was covered with dried gray blossoms. They circled the fire, chanting louder and louder until they were all howling and dancing. They panted and sweated in the heat and effort. Their eyes were open wide, glazed, unseeing.

As the fire went down, they slowed. Each in turn then emptied the contents of his pouch on the coals.

A thick blue smoke rose, tobacco and some other herb Andrew had not smelled before.

The priests fanned this smoke over Mr. Harriot's body, moaning low together as if singing a lullaby. Some of the smoke drifted over Andrew. Suddenly he felt as if he were floating.

When the fire was out, the priests carried the litter to the house of the dead and shoved it in.

Andrew felt like he'd been kicked in the stomach.

"Manteo!" he cried. "Is he dead?" The boy was weeping.

"Wait!" said Manteo. He was like one in a trance.

"Is he alive?"

Manteo nodded slowly. The smoke had affected him too.

"What did they smoke him with?"

Manteo shook his head. "Go now," he said. "Come tomorrow afternoon. I will watch him with Sky."

"What will Captain Lane do when he finds out?" Andrew asked as he and Tremayne rowed back to the fort together.

"Depends on whether Mr. Harriot is alive or dead, doesn't it?" Tremayne replied. "We've done what we could, and what we've done is right!"

When they returned the next afternoon, Mr. Harriot was lying in the sun. He was still on the stretcher, but he was conscious. His fever had broken. Manteo and Sky sat beside him.

Andrew whispered, "Thank you. Your people saved him."

Manteo nodded but said nothing.

"What did they smoke him with?" Andrew asked again. "And the dried flowers they put over his body— what were they?"

Manteo shook his head.

"In the spring I'll show you," Sky promised later. "The flowers and the seeds they threw on the fire are from the same plant. It is the priest's chant, though— their prayer—that gives it power."

"Why do you teach me these things when your uncle will not?" Andrew asked.

"Because we are brothers. You teach me what you call your science; I teach you ours. We can do much together!"

Mr. Harriot lay weak for days. He remembered nothing.

The captain asked no questions. Somehow he'd got word. That night he read aloud to the company from Saint Mark about men casting out devils, speaking with new tongues, and taking up serpents.

34
CHRISTMAS REVELS AT FORT ROANOKE

The winter moon was like a pearl in blue velvet, bright against soft, large and indistinct, charmed. The first dustings of snow revealed every path. Seeds, dried leaves, branches, and twigs appeared like sea wrack on the white crust. In the clear, slanted morning light, larch needles in bared places came up the color of old pottery. As the woods grew lighter without the leaves, the spruce, rhododendron, and pines glowed green. The hideout Andrew had built with Sky was visible to everyone now. The men said it was a bear's nest.

There was still some cricket song, some gold and yellow in the woods; then it was winter proper. Two weeks before Christmas, a major blowing storm broke off branches and left deep drifts.

The air took on a dry spice smell as the storm cleared and the sky turned rose. While the company shoveled, made snowmen, and tossed snowballs, Andrew helped the carpenters build simple two-man sleds—heavy crude planks with wooden runners. There was no steering them—you just aimed and went. The men trooped out to the gully to race, yelling and laughing as they shot down the steep that got slicker and slicker with every run until it was sheer ice and there were crashes and bruises. That night they all sang songs and danced jigs in front of the fort's great stone fireplace. Firewood was one thing they had plenty of.

Andrew wore Pena's cap for America day and night now. Every time he put it on, his breath caught as he pictured his burly friend in the garden at Durham House.

With the needle Mr. Harriot had given him, Sky stitched a cap like Andrew's from the skins of rabbits they snared. They played hide-and-seek in the winter woods. Andrew gave Sky a mirror and taught him how to flash and signal in the bright cold light.

No one dared grumble within earshot of Captain Lane, but he knew his people were dismayed that food was short and they'd not found gold. To keep order, he worked the explorers harder than ever gathering firewood, strengthening the fort, surveying, hunting. "Not so glum, my boys!" he said over and over. "Work cures all dismay."

The day of the snowstorm, he summoned Mr. Harriot.

"You must plan our revels!" he announced. "We'll be wanting skits and music. Work it up."

The carpenters built a makeshift stage in the great hall with a sign: "Fort Roanoke revels, 1585." Chief Pemisapan and his dignitaries were invited. They came in full warrior regalia with gifts of tobacco. The English put on their fineries too, including the gentleman whose yellow silk suit got stained in the *Tyger's* grounding. The Indians admired him most of all: "Yellow bird!" they said in their language, pointing and nodding as the firelight caught their oiled faces and made them gleam in a way that made some uneasy.

To warm things up, the Englishmen sang patriotic songs and the Queen's anthem, everyone playing and banging away on something—bagpipes, whistles, rattles, battle drums, bells, flutes, fiddles. Then it was time for the skit. They built the fire up to roaring and lit torches. The place went silent. The air was thick with blue tobacco smoke.

To a merry march of bagpipes and fiddles, Sky flashed a mirror beam on a figure dressed like a young

warrior creeping out from a dark corner toward someone dressed like Captain Lane, in armor and tin hat, with a heavy stick in one hand, a shovel in the other. As the warrior drew close, the captain banged his stick on the floor and waved the shovel. "Dig, boys, dig! Dig harder!" he yelled.

The Indians in the audience nudged one another, pointing first at the warrior, then at the captain. "Big Thumps-a-Stick!" they muttered.

Andrew played the Indian; Tremayne played Captain Lane. It took a while for the noisy captain to notice the boy. When at last he did, he thumped and stomped even harder.

"What do you dig for?" the warrior asked.

"Gold!" the captain thundered. "Grains of gold!"

"You look hungry, sir. Do you eat those grains?"

"Ignorance!" the captain spluttered.

"We grow yellow grains you can eat!" the warrior announced. "Would you like me to show you?"

The captain turned away, reciting Bible verses at the top of his voice.

The Indian put up his hands and made a sad face as he turned away.

The captain stood tall as he held out the shovel. "Not so glum, my boy! Work cures all dismay!"

As the company roared its pleasure, the actors stood in the shadows.

What would Captain Lane say?

Sky shined the mirror on the captain as he stepped forward, clapping and bowing to Andrew and Tremayne.

"A dram of spirits for everyone in the house!" he ordered. The strong drink sent the Indians staggering as the explorers toasted the players, the captain, Sir Walter, and the Queen.

On a signal from the captain, the English sang grace with more feeling than one might have expected from that rowdy crowd, then sat down to feast on bear meat none too fresh. They were merry, but their guts were as noisy and windy as the bagpipes.

After the feast there were more jigs and reels, men dancing with men as their Indian guests looked on. When at last the company was tired and sweaty, there were carols, and Mr. Harriot read the Christmas story from Luke.

Then the presents! A gold angel coin from Sir Walter for each of the men; a fine French knife for Sky—"So the next time you cut me, you won't have to use an oyster shell," the captain laughed. Andrew got the same. There were compasses for Wanchese and Manteo; for Tremayne and Mr. Harriot, Spanish pistols.

There were knitted wool caps for the Indians, which they wouldn't put on but held open like sacks, hoping for better. At last, to a skreel of bagpipes and rattle of battle drums, Mr. Harriot made Chief Pemisapan the gift of a spring clock. Its ticking and the moving hands enchanted the chief. The metal was alive!

"You will thrive so long as the clock's hands turn," Mr. Harriot advised. "If they slow or stop, you must send to the fort." Mr. Harriot kept the key.

There was a surprise to conclude all. At Mr. Harriot's directing, Sky had helped Tremayne and Andrew tie bags of gunpowder to the branches of a large tree opposite the gate. When all the explorers were gathered outside, bidding farewell to their guests, a snake of flame shot sizzling from the fort. With a roar, the tree appeared to rise up out of the ground, exploding in yellow, blue, and red flashes.

The Indians and many of the English threw themselves on the ground in terror. They got up professing it a great joke.

The day after Christmas, a party of warriors came to the fort with corn, venison, and fish, enough for one hundred four men. Chief Pemisapan's clock had stopped.

35

FOR GOLD AND THE PACIFIC SEA

It was late. Andrew rubbed his eyes. He'd been copying for an hour; his hand was stained and sore. He'd just written Mr. Harriot's estimate of how much food they had left in the fort.

Tremayne had been sitting with them, adding comments and corrections. Now he stood and stretched.

"We send to the Indians every other day now," he muttered. "Pemisapan gives as little as he can. Only for fear of our guns does he give anything."

Mr. Harriot nodded. "He's had enough of us, burning glasses, copper pots, flaming trees, and clocks no matter. At this rate we'll soon be eating what they need to plant in the spring."

Wanchese was listening. "Chief Pemisapan says it is strange," he said, "that the white men's god gives them pistols and spinning needles but lets them starve."

"Tell the chief our God provided him to care for us," said Mr. Harriot, looking hard at Wanchese.

The Indian looked away.

Every morning now the captain would send a team of explorers fanning out through the forest to drive game toward the hunters. Others gathered crabs and forked for oysters.

Sky showed Andrew how to gather small seeds from a dried plant that stuck up through the snow. It took all morning to gather a cupful, which they pounded into paste and baked into small cakes. Some days, that and a few oysters were all they ate.

Manteo showed them how to make a bread of acorns pounded and shelled, with some of the bitterness leached out in salt water. Andrew could not eat it for the cramp it gave his guts, but Mr. Harriot declared it tastier than English bread.

"We've learned to eat hunger," Tremayne joked, but even as they grew gaunt, the greatest hunger among the explorers was still for gold. The hungriest of all was the captain.

Ever since his first meeting with Chief Pemisapan, Captain Lane had made it clear he wanted wassador more than anything. The chief, for his part, soon realized he did not have enough saved corn to feed everyone through the winter and plant in the spring.

Mr. Harriot was in charge of the next party that rowed across the channel to trade for food. When he was settled in the chief's lodge, Pemisapan surprised him with news about a large village five days' paddle to the north, near the great bay the Indians called Chesapeake.

"We trade with their chief, Menatonon," Pemisapan said. "Skins for metal. They will give your chief news of wassador." Mr. Harriot pressed Pemisapan to say more. He wouldn't. That day the explorers got less corn and moldier.

Captain Lane clapped his hands when he heard about the village the wassador had come from. Mr. Harriot looked brighter than he had since his illness. They asked Manteo and Wanchese about it. Wanchese shook his head and said nothing.

"It used to be they could send seven hundred warriors to battle," Manteo reported. "Now I don't know."

"Our guns would be nothing against so many," the captain mused. "We must devise a trick. What can you tell me about their chief? You, Manteo, what do you know about him?"

"He is weak in his limbs from fever," Manteo replied. "His favorite son carries him."

"Ah," said the captain, lowering his eyes as he nodded to himself.

"Do you know about this tribe?" Andrew asked Sky later.

"No. And I never heard where the metal came from. I thought it came from the god Okeus."

On Valentine's Day in wet snow, Tremayne, Mr. Harriot, and Andrew mustered with the captain and a small company to go to Chief Menatonon's village.

Andrew whispered to Mr. Harriot, "Can Sky come along?"

"No!" said Mr. Harriot, making a grim face. "But for Sir Walter's order, the captain would leave you behind too."

Sky knew without being told. He was not around when Andrew went to say goodbye. He'd gone back to his home island.

As they proceeded up the river valley, Mr. Harriot measured how fast the water fell. "This will be a good place for mills," he observed, sketching a map. "Close to meadows where we can grow grain and not far from the sound for shipping."

As the company approached Chief Menatonon's village, Captain Lane sent Wanchese ahead with two soldiers to arrange a parley.

"Tell him I come to speak."

Word came back that the English were welcome. Chief Menatonon would meet Captain Lane in front of his lodge.

The captain wore his heavy cape with large pockets. Mr. Harriot and Andrew walked just behind him to translate.

The chief sat propped on a litter. Although it was raw and blowing rain, all he wore was a patch at his waist and a deerskin about his shoulders. His legs and arms were withered.

His allegiance men and favorite son stood beside him. As Captain Lane's party approached, Menatonon's people came out from their lodges. They showed no fear.

Captain Lane walked up slowly, holding his hands out, palms up.

Menatonon nodded slightly.

"Give him our greeting," the captain ordered Mr. Harriot. Captain Lane slipped his hands into his pockets as if they were cold.

Mr. Harriot had just started his speech of greeting

when the captain drew a pistol from his cloak and fired it into the ground before the chief's litter. The shot sent up clods of mud and dirt. As the Indians fell back yelling, the captain drew another pistol from his pocket and pointed it at Menatonon's head.

"Mr. Harriot!" he snarled. "Tell his men I'll shoot him if they attack."

Andrew stood frightened, trying to understand. Then his face began to burn.

Before Mr. Harriot could speak, Menatonon signaled his men to stand back. He was calm, almost amused by the trick. He tilted his head a little as if to ask, "What do you want?"

The captain summoned his soldiers to bind the crippled man's hands.

Andrew shrank away from the captain. He looked at Mr. Harriot. The tall man was pale, his mouth tight with anger. *We are just like Spaniards,* Andrew thought.

"Wanchese," the captain ordered. "Ask him where the wassador is."

There was a pause. Chief Menatonon seemed bewildered, unable to understand the question. At last he replied, "There is a great river to the north. Where it falls out of the mountains, men take grains of metal from the sand."

The captain held up one of the medals he'd taken from the sacred cave. "Is the metal like this?" he asked, thrusting it in the chief's face.

Menatonon stared. "Where did you get that?" he whispered.

"Why? What is it?" Mr. Harriot asked.

"The image of our god Okeus. Only the chief priest has such a thing."

"What's he saying? What's he saying?" Captain Lane demanded.

"Skip all that!" the captain ordered when Mr. Harriot told him. "Wanchese," he said, motioning Mr. Harriot aside, "ask him if the grains they find where the water falls out of the mountain are hard or soft."

The chief was calm. He closed his eyes as if dozing. Andrew's face was still hot with shame.

"Well?" the captain barked, stamping his foot.

"Soft."

The captain narrowed his eyes and nodded. "So! Perhaps we'll find gold there.

"And beyond the headwaters of that river, is there a great sea? Ask him that, Wanchese!"

"Over the smoke-colored mountains, much water" was the reply.

"The Pacific!" the captain cried. "We've discovered a passage to the East—a way to China!" He couldn't contain himself. "How far is it to the headwaters?" he spluttered. "Ask him that, Wanchese: how far is it to the headwaters of that river?"

The captain was pacing about, impatient with how long it took Wanchese to ask his questions and how slow the drowsy chief was to answer.

Andrew was afraid of what the captain would do. The man seemed crazed. The boy held his breath as he watched the captain feel for the pistol.

Wanchese could not seem to make the chief understand.

"You, Mr. Harriot, you ask him how far it is to the place where the river begins," the captain bellowed. He was clasping and unclasping his hands. His face was bright with sweat.

Mr. Harriot whispered to the chief.

There was a long pause. Again the captain stomped. The chief's eyes were closed. The captain fumbled with his pistol.

"Fifteen days, twenty," the chief replied at last.

"And how many days beyond the mountains to the sea?"

Andrew watched as the chief seemed to doze off. He wasn't faking; he was fainting.

"The same," Menatonon said finally.

"Ask him if he's been there, Mr. Harriot."

Andrew studied the chief's face and chest as Mr. Harriot questioned him. Everything about the Indian slowed as if he was dying. Then, with a huge effort, he roused himself.

"No."

"Then how does he get metal to trade with Chief Pemisapan? Do you understand, Wanchese? I want to know how he gets metal to trade for skins."

"We trade for it with the mountain people" was the reply.

Captain Lane was desperate to get to where the grains of soft metal were found, then on to the Pacific Ocean, but first he had to return to base and make preparations.

"We'll take Menatonon with us as hostage so his people don't attack us as we go," he announced.

"That may prove too much for him," Mr. Harriot warned. "If he dies on the way, we're dead men too."

Manteo suggested they exchange the chief for Skiko, the chief's favorite son.

"Make the exchange," the captain muttered.

Skiko went with them back to Fort Roanoke, manacled to one of the company day and night. He was Tremayne's age. He made no complaint as the irons chafed at his wrists and ankles. While he was chained to Tremayne, Andrew cut strips of hide and cloth to cushion Skiko's hurts, but they didn't help. The wounds became infected. By the time they arrived at the fort, his wrists and ankles were red and swollen, oozing pus. Andrew treated them with salt water.

The captain called a meeting of his council. Mr. Harriot ordered Andrew to take notes. "Write down as much of it as you can get," he said.

"We have three choices," the captain announced. "We may stay here and starve, racking our guts on their moldy corn. Or we can attempt to move our fort to a better harbor on the Chesapeake. Or we can try for gold and the Pacific Sea.

"If we set out now, we could be back by Easter— in time to meet the supply Sir Walter promised.

"What do you say?"

To a man, they shouted, "For gold and the Pacific Sea!"

The captain's face was red as a drunk's.

"Excellent! Excellent! We'll divide . . . divide the company," he stammered in his excitement. "Forty of the strongest to go, sixty to stay."

At that there were loud grumbles.

"No fear!" he yelled. "Spoils and treasure will be shared equal among all."

Late into the night, he worked out details of

the expedition with his lieutenants. Mr. Harriot, Tremayne, and Andrew observed but said nothing.

"We will go with what we need for a week," he told them. "Thereafter we'll supply ourselves, trading or raiding as we travel—copper pots or lead shot, their choice," he said with a harsh laugh.

"Pemisapan must not know," the captain added in a hushed voice. "He must believe the whole company is here, sending for food as usual."

After writing in the log for Mr. Harriot, Andrew told Sky what had happened.

"Captain Lane broke his honor," Sky said. "He traded his spirit for the bright metal."

Before dawn on Ash Wednesday, the captain slipped out of the fort with a small company plus two mastiffs as guard dogs. He left Skiko behind in chains as hostage. It was cold and drizzling. Andrew pulled on his cap for America.

"You look like a suffering monk in that," the captain teased.

Andrew looked at the captain's hat, already sopping. "Perhaps, sir, but mine sheds wet."

There were snickers. Captain Lane shot Andrew an ugly look that made the boy afraid.

36

STEW OF DOG

It was slow, cold going as they poled the heavy boats upriver. Andrew went ahead with the scouts, looking for signs of life. "A village!" he reported to Mr. Harriot. "But no smoke, no people."

They stopped and searched. The fires had been cold for days. "There's not a grain of corn to be found," Tremayne announced. Andrew shivered. The place smelled dead.

The second village they came to was the same. Every village they came to was dead to them.

"This must be by plan," Mr. Harriot said. "The people have been sent off. Not even the old and sick remain."

Their meals now amounted to a half-pint measure of corn each day. They grubbed for roots, made stew of sassafras, and chewed buds like the deer. Salt ate where he killed. He knew if he came near the men, he'd be robbed.

After a week without meat, the two mastiffs they'd brought as guards were starving. Their once-fine brindle coats hung slack on their great bodies. Their eyes were dull. They smelled ill. They no longer had strength to clean themselves.

One afternoon Manteo motioned to Andrew. "I feel eyes," he whispered. "We're being watched." Andrew's hair went up. He felt eyes too.

Early the next morning, Manteo surprised a young warrior. As the boy sprinted away, he tripped on a root and twisted his ankle. Manteo caught him.

"He does not talk," he said when he reported to the captain.

The prisoner was a little older than Andrew, perhaps fourteen. There was no fear in his eyes. They were bright and hard.

Captain Lane called Wanchese to interrogate. He didn't come. The men looked around. Wanchese was gone!

Andrew had never seen the captain surprised.

"Then you!" he ordered Manteo. "Ask him why the people have fled. Find out where they have gone."

"He does not talk," Manteo said again.

The captain ordered torture. He had a man shave slivers of pine in front of the Indian and gesture how they would be driven deep under his fingernails and set afire.

Watching that show made Andrew angry. "Would Sir Walter do this?" he asked Mr. Harriot.

The tall man looked hard at him and nodded. "To keep us safe he would. He's a soldier first, above all."

As the Indian boy watched the preparations for his torture, his eyes glazed over as if his mind were leaving his body.

"It's no good," said Manteo. "Torture will not make him talk. But the mastiffs might. Bring up the dogs."

The warrior had never seen such dogs. The handlers brought them close, growling and foaming. In his terror they got from him that Pemisapan had sent messengers to the river villages: "The white ones come to destroy you," they warned. "Take your food and leave! Starve them."

"How did Pemisapan learn our plan?" Captain Lane asked.

"From the one who fled," Mr. Harriot said quietly. "Wanchese betrayed us."

Or we betrayed him, Andrew thought.

Captain Lane's face worked for a moment, his mouth pulled tight.

He called the company together. "We have two pints of corn per man," he said in an even voice. "I figure we are one hundred sixty miles from Fort Roanoke, four or five days' travel downriver. We can turn back now," he said slowly, "or"—his voice deepening—"we can go on to the place where the grains of metal are found."

Although many were sick from hunger, all but two voted to go on.

"Good!" exclaimed the captain. "You are good men!"

He ordered the captive bound to a tree by the river. The boy's foot was swollen, bluish gray. Andrew caught his eyes as they left. The Indian's sought nothing.

"Tremayne," Andrew whispered, "we can't leave him."

"He would leave you."

"He'll die there," Andrew said, his face tightening as he imagined the boy's pain and terror.

"Probably," the man said quietly. He studied Andrew, then put an arm around him. "There's nothing we can do. We have to make sure we don't die here! Come on!"

Two days later, the handlers strung the mastiffs

up like hogs and cut their throats. They saved the blood. They boiled the butchered dogs in blood and sassafras.

That day, the company ate pottage of dog spiced with sassafras. At first Andrew gagged; then he ate and felt better for it. His mind was numb.

37

PEMISAPAN'S LAST PLOT

Andrew lay half awake in the first light. Hunger prodded him. His mind raced in the way hunger inspires.

Wanchese and Pemisapan scheme to starve us on the river. Once they know we're dead, they're going to kill those left at the fort. Wanchese has gone to Pemisapan to do that work!

He poked Tremayne awake and told him what he'd figured out. "Wanchese is an allegiance man," Andrew explained. "Pemisapan wants us gone. Wanchese follows his plan."

"Yes, it's possible, Wanchese going off like that . . . ," Tremayne said slowly. "What do we do? How do we get word to the fort?"

Just then Salt made a row after a squirrel that had slipped under a log. Thinking to eat that breakfast for him, Andrew heaved at the log and went sprawling.

It was a small hollowed-log boat with two rough paddles.

Tremayne looked at Andrew and nodded. "That's how we'll beat Wanchese!" he said with a tight smile.

They went and told Mr. Harriot. Together they examined the boat. "It might work," Mr. Harriot muttered. "It's worth anything to try and beat Pemisapan. Let's see what the captain says."

"I wouldn't have Andrew tell it the way he told it to me," Tremayne said. "It sounds too much like a dream."

"You two tell him, then," Andrew replied.

Mr. Harriot went to Captain Lane. Without mentioning Andrew, he reported what Andrew had figured Wanchese was up to and their plan to beat him to the fort.

The captain's jaw worked when he heard the Indian's name. Slowly, he nodded. "Show me the boat," he said after a pause.

"It will carry you three," he muttered when he saw it. "Go, and good luck!" He turned quickly and walked away.

As they dropped down the river, Andrew watched for the place where they'd left the young captive.

He wasn't there. Nobody said anything. A weight lifted from Andrew's heart.

They paddled without stop, switching places as they went, two paddling as the one resting ate cold stew of dog, cooled his blistered hands, and scooped water from the river. The ache in their shoulders became a steady searing flame of pain.

It was almost dark when Salt stiffened. They smelled smoke. They hardly breathed as they drifted past.

In the fire's glow they saw Wanchese, his back to them.

They paddled all that night and through the next day. It was dark when they beached the boat on the shore below the fort and stumbled up to the gate. It was barred.

As Salt barked their greeting, Mr. Harriot yelled, "What cheer, Englishmen! Admit us!"

They could hear calling inside. Suddenly a clutch of flaming reeds came flying over the rampart. The three moved close to the burning reeds so the guards could see their faces.

"It's Mr. Harriot!" someone shouted. "Open the gate! It's Mr. Harriot with Tremayne and Andrew!"

As they entered the fort, folks rushed up, pulling on clothes and yelling, "Where are the others?" "Did you find gold?"

"Wanchese betrayed us," Mr. Harriot said, and downed a dram of spirits to ease the pain in his shoulders. "He plotted with Pemisapan to starve us," he went on as he filled the glass for Tremayne. "All the river villages were deserted. Once Wanchese figured we were sure to die of hunger in the cold, he hurried back to help attack the weakened fort. We passed him last night. He'll make Pemisapan's village tomorrow."

Tremayne left something in the glass for Andrew. It burned going down, but soon it soothed.

"The others were alive when we left them," Mr. Harriot continued. "They're a day or two behind us. We never got to where the wassador is found.

"And you people? Your news?"

"We are as you left us, sir, only starker," replied the lieutenant. "The last time we sent to Pemisapan for food, he turned us away with nothing. He lets time do his work."

"The hostage, Skiko, how is he?" Mr. Harriot asked.

"He's well."

The people at Fort Roanoke had kept Skiko fed and comfortable, despite their own wants.

Mr. Harriot went to him. "I'm sorry," he said as he unlocked Skiko's chains.

The Indian said nothing. He left the next morning with a large tin platter, a peace offering for his father.

The following afternoon Captain Lane and the haggard expedition men straggled in. Right away, the captain set off with Mr. Harriot, Tremayne, and Andrew and an armed guard to parley with Pemisapan for food and show the chief his plan was spoiled.

Andrew watched Pemisapan's face as they filed into his lodge. If the chief was startled to see them alive, he gave no sign. Andrew noticed that the allegiance men, though, studied them as rare creatures.

Their surviving seemed to convince Pemisapan they really were possessed of a kind of magic. That, plus the power of their guns, persuaded him to allow the English a measure of his seed corn and the promise his people would plant two fields for them.

It was dark when they got back to the fort. Captain Lane addressed the company: "Pemisapan has sold us food for three days. He will continue to buy our pots, cloth, and other goods. For pleasure in those things and fear of our guns, he promises to have his people plant for us."

"If that's all there is, we can't last," Tremayne murmured to Andrew. "The new corn won't be ripe until

July." Andrew belched a dry heave and wondered if the taste in his mouth was fear. His stomach rumbled.

Tremayne heard and nodded. "Mine too," he said gently. "Never mind. We'll make it. Sir Walter knows we're hungry. The resupply he promised for Easter is out there somewhere." Besides cheering Andrew, Tremayne cheered himself.

The next evening Andrew wrote in the journal, "We eat so little now we enjoy great cleanness of teeth."

As he was writing, Skiko returned with a warning. Andrew translated for the company: "I have been to see Pemisapan. He treats me as an ally because I was your prisoner. A great priest has died. Pemisapan has summoned a large gathering of mourners, mostly warriors. They will assemble at his village. He has been buying alliances with them with your copper pots.

"When the moon is down, he'll bring those warriors here in boats. On a signal, his allegiance men will shoot fire arrows into the captain's house and Mr. Harriot's. When you come rushing out in your nightshirts, they will slaughter you and then take on the whole, which he says will be no more dangerous than a headless snake."

As Andrew reported Skiko's message, Captain

Lane began to pace. He narrowed his eyes and glared at Skiko. "Ask him why he warns us. It may be a trick."

Andrew repeated exactly what the captain had said.

Skiko gave the captain a long look. "For the care your men and those two took of me," he said finally, pointing to Andrew and Tremayne. "The mourners come soon," he warned as he left.

The captain called the company together. "We are doomed if we wait. The only thing for it is to strike first.

"Now!

"We'll need to be few and quick: me, my ten best soldiers, and you, Mr. Harriot, to lead us through Pemisapan's village—you know it best and can do our interrogating.

"Who else?" he said, half to himself. Andrew held his breath; he didn't want to be left out.

"Andrew," said Mr. Harriot. "He has the naphtha and knows how to manage it. Better than fire arrows— he can set the main lodges afire all at once. Tremayne will lay the fuse."

"Yes!" said the captain. "Fourteen people; three boats."

The attackers blackened their faces. Andrew half-smiled to himself at how cold his hands were as he smeared on the wood ash. His face was hot.

They canoed to the mainland. The sky was dark; there was a noisy wind. Andrew carried a large piece of flint, the piece of roughened steel to strike against, and the bottle of naphtha. Tremayne carried the fuse—a long rope of cotton cloth laced with gunpowder. The boy's only thought was how the village was laid out, where the lodges he had to spread the naphtha around were. He checked the bottle. Tight. He patted his pocket to make sure the flint and steel were there. *Yes.*

The raiders slipped into the village, tossing bones to the dogs. The captain's scouts crept up behind the Indian guards, flung silk cords around their necks and pulled tight, then bagged the heads in canvas sacks.

Andrew rubbed his hands together to warm them so his grip would be good on the naphtha bottle. As Tremayne set out to lay the fuse, Andrew crept around the lodges where Pemisapan and his allegiance men slept. He tried to pour an even band. The smell was strong. He held his breath when he heard people stirring inside. Now he was panting, but his hands were steady. His only thought was to spread the naphtha right, no breaks, around here, there, and then a trail to where the fuse would be.

With the last of it, he made a pool, where Tremayne set the fuse end.

Calm now, staring, listening hard, Andrew slipped to his place of safety.

At the captain's yell, he struck a spark. It didn't take. His hands were shaking. He struck again. Too feeble. "Steady!" he said to himself. "Steady." It was Sir Walter's voice. "One, two, three—strike!"

The fuse caught. It burned toward the lodges faster than a man could run.

Andrew hadn't realized it, but in his nervousness he'd spilled some of the naphtha on his boot. As the fuse caught, the spark had set him on fire too!

Struggling to stifle his own flames, he watched the fuse fire flashing and sparking to where the naphtha started.

"Yes!" he shouted when the naphtha caught. It went around the lodges exactly right, fiercer and higher than he'd expected, first firing the lodge coverings, then the whole in a crackling roar as black smoke billowed up out of the orange.

"Yes!" he shouted again, weaker, as he heard screams and felt the sear of his own burns.

Amidst yells and gunshots, Pemisapan fled in the confusion of frantic men, women, and children. No one stayed behind to fight; the Indians disappeared into the forest as their village went up like an immense bonfire. The flames cast evil shapes over the cornfields. It was like the painting of hell in the Queen's gallery.

Andrew's foot was agony now, cooked like a sausage. He tried to walk. He couldn't. He pulled off what remained of his boot.

His foot was blistering up in large white welts when Captain Lane and the other English scouring the village for holdouts began whistling and cheering. Andrew's mouth dropped open as one of the soldiers appeared in the awful firelight, holding something away from his body.

It was Pemisapan's head, dangling crooked from his hair knot, the face ghastly, torn, smiling.

The boy retched as he saw Tremayne following, holding up the breastplate of wassador.

Mr. Harriot found Andrew. He was on the ground, his shoulders shaking like one sobbing. It wasn't just pain.

"Better him than us," Mr. Harriot muttered.

"Two injured, not one Englishman lost," the captain

bellowed, looking around as he kicked at the smoking ruin of Pemisapan's lodge. "They won't be back!"

"I guess not," Tremayne said quietly. "We just burned up the last of their saved corn." He buttoned the plate of wassador inside his shirt.

Mr. Harriot and Tremayne helped Andrew back to their boat. At the fort, Mr. Harriot gave him a drop of Sir Walter's opium tincture. The boy went down like the Frenchman at Marseilles.

38

ATTACK OR RESCUE?

The next morning, Sky returned from his home island. He knew everything about the attack. He brought Andrew a paste he'd made from the stems and roots of a large-leaved plant with white flowers. It calmed the burn enough that Andrew could hobble.

"I snared two rabbits for us," Sky said. "We'll roast them in the gully. No one will smell and ask to share."

He'd showed Andrew the snares. They were hoops of grass so slight they barely made a shadow.

When they got to the gully, Sky gutted the rabbits. As he flicked out the innards, Salt snapped and swallowed them in midair. Sky pulled his needle from the cord around his neck and a strand of silk grass from the pouch at his waist. He sewed the belly skins back tight. "We roast them in their skins," he said. "Saves the juice!"

As the two boys ate, Salt munched the bones to nothing, then settled happily to gnaw the heads.

"We killed him," Andrew said slowly. He pinched his lips together. "We were going to be friends and make them Christians. For a while he did what he could for us. . . ."

"You had to," Sky replied. "You heard what Skiko said."

"We made him do it," Andrew said. "If the *Tyger* hadn't sunk, it would all be different."

Sky looked at his friend. "It's not your fault. What could you do? And if you'd been the captain, would you have done different?"

"That's about what Mr. Harriot said," Andrew replied. "I asked him if Sir Walter would have done the same. 'To keep us safe he would. He's a soldier above all' was his answer."

May in that land was like spring in Devon, with wild white roses scenting the air, the green shading darker with every rain, and overnight new leaves sprouting on the brush like mouse ears. In a sunny place, a square-stemmed mint put forth a fist of red flowers. Birds no larger than English moths came hovering to sip them. There were mats of moss thick and soft as velvet pillows. Green scum formed on the ponds; in shallow places frogs laid eggs.

Every day, Captain Lane sent teams of scouts and hunters to the mainland, looking for food and signs of Indians gathering to attack. "No people," they reported back. "Little game."

Andrew and Sky spent most of their time hunting food too. Sky showed Andrew new shoots to eat and tubers of something he called groundnuts. They gave Andrew the cramp, but he fed better than some.

The captain worked the men harder than ever to keep them from despair. The moat was dug deeper, the fort strengthened, huge piles of wood were gathered along the shore for bonfires to welcome the relief he assured them would arrive any day.

"All will be well," he said. "The supply will come and you'll grow fat again. You will tell your children and grandchildren about this place. Some of you will come back to stay!"

He ordered the watch kept day and night for Indians and Spaniards. Relays of scouts checked the mainland. They saw no one.

Since his first visit to Pemisapan's village, Andrew had been curious about the medicine root the priests placed on the beds of their dead in the burial lodges and chewed for food on their long trips.

"We gather it now," Sky explained. "When the hot days come, the leaves die off and you cannot find it."

They had just dug a clump in the woods along the shore when they heard hollering.

"We are discovered!" gasped a half-dead runner from the farthest watch. His legs were bloody from falls and scrapes. "Many sails! Spaniards come to clear us out! Run! Warn them!"

Andrew and Sky raced to the fort.

The captain ordered all the bonfires lit to make the Spaniards think the English had a great force on the island. He had the signal mirrors flashed and the fort's bell rung to call folks in.

The boys ran to their tree house and hauled up. The line of ships stretched longer and longer as they watched.

"If they're Spanish, I'll take you to my village," Sky murmured.

"If they're Spanish, we'll fight them off or die rolling in our blood!" Andrew replied.

A half hour later the second of the three watchers staggered up to the fort, his boots gone, his face torn from stumbling into brambles.

"They show the flag of St. George! They are English or pirates pretending to be English!" he said, panting.

The third watchman followed soon after, crying as he stumbled, "English! Admiral Drake's ensign! His fleet!"

By now the captain could make them out through Mr. Harriot's glass.

"Flash the mirrors to signal welcome!" he ordered. "Row us out!"

"I can't take you along," Andrew whispered to Sky.

"I know," the Indian said with a wry smile.

Andrew looked at him, then looked away.

The flagship's name was carved on her stern, *Elizabeth Bonaventure.* At her prow she bore a great golden figure representing the Queen.

As Captain Lane and his people rowed up, the *Elizabeth*'s pilot yelled, "Where are your harbor marks?"

"There is no harbor!" bellowed Captain Lane. "Stay deep or you'll go aground!"

Sir Francis stood on the deck to greet them, a burly, smiling, round-faced man with a broad red beard.

"I've come at Sir Walter's request to find how you

do," he said by way of greeting. His voice was strong and clear. Andrew liked him from the start!

"On our way here, we sacked the Spanish fort to the south at St. Augustine," the admiral continued. "They will do you no mischief now."

"Thank you, sir," said Captain Lane as he clambered aboard, "but our present enemy is hunger. The promised resupply has failed us, and things do not go well with the Indians. We need to move but we have no fit vessel."

Sir Francis was not one to hesitate.

"I will supply you," he said with a firm nod. "Food for a year and the *Francis,* a vessel small enough to manage your shoals and bars yet large enough to move you to a better place on the Chesapeake."

"This is Christmas, truly!" said the captain with a bow.

"Ah!" said Sir Francis, beaming. "Perhaps you and your best people will join me tonight in my cabin for supper? We'll toast the Queen and her explorers!"

"We'd be honored," said the captain. "I'll send out a crew to transfer supplies and bring in the *Francis.*"

The guests went back to wash and put on their finest. Andrew unfolded his page's outfit. He hadn't put it on since leaving Durham House. There were moth holes in the jacket. It was tight. The sleeves were short.

Sky watched him dress. "You are not Andrew now," he said quietly.

"Who am I, then?" Andrew asked with a surprised laugh.

"Allegiance man to Sir Walter."

"Perhaps you will become one too?" Andrew said, looking closely at his friend.

"No," said Sky, shaking his head. "I am an Indian. I cannot become a Raleigh English, just as you cannot become one of us."

"Andrew! To the boat!" Tremayne yelled.

Andrew avoided Sky's eyes as he left.

Everyone wore such finery as he had, except Mr. Harriot. He wore what he always wore: his long black coat.

Admiral Drake's cabin smelled of clove and glowed with polished rosewood, bright rubbed brass, beeswax candles, decanters of gold-colored wine, platters of roast pork. The food was served on shining plates. The party stood and cheered the Queen, Sir Walter, Sir Francis, and Captain Lane.

"And Virginia!" called Mr. Harriot. "A toast for her! She'll outlast all!"

Folks yelled and drummed their boots. Andrew sat still; his burned foot was still sore.

39

HURRICANE!

"There will be a great storm," Manteo warned.

"How can you tell?" Mr. Harriot asked.

"No fish come in. I feel a strange rising in my hair."

Captain Lane's picked crew was out on the *Francis,* transferring supplies from the *Elizabeth Bonaventure.* There was no time to warn them. The freak weather came up fast under a yellow sky, with thunder, lightning, tearing winds, and jagged pieces of ice large as grapes. As the winds gained force, branches and small trees shot past like cannon fire on the hailing winds.

They'd had gales and storms on the island before, winds that had laid the marsh reeds flat and chewed up trees straggling to grow along the water's edge. This was different: the spears of lightning were huge and lingering. The winds blew fierce from one quarter, then turned to attack from another. There was no safety anywhere.

"Woe for the ships out there!" Mr. Harriot yelled as sheets of rain and hail whipped through Drake's fleet, tossing vessels like leaves.

"Woe for us!" Tremayne shouted back as part of the log wall they were huddled against gave way.

Andrew and Sky clung to each other, shivering in Andrew's coat. Salt lay buried in the boy's blanket.

It raged wind and rain all that day and night, the water sounding like the sea coming down on them, the wind screaming and making eerie whistles as it caught in corners. At one moment the air blew warm, the next cold.

With a thundering crash, the huge tree they'd hung with bags of gunpowder at Christmas toppled into the fort. It was open to Spaniards now. Spaniards they could fight; there was no defending against the killer storm. All was chaos, noise, and wet. The moat was frothing foam and whitecaps.

Toward dawn it grew still, then cleared to cloudless blue. Birds sang. The air was pungent with the smell of shredded cedar.

The boys helped Mr. Harriot climb up to their tree house. He searched the water with his glass.

The ships were scattered.

"Sixteen, seventeen, eighteen . . ."

He got to twenty-two.

"One's missing!" he exclaimed.

He was scanning the coast for wreckage when he picked up a dot on the horizon.

It was the *Francis,* making for England under all the sail she had left—their exploring ship with Captain Lane's picked crew, the resupply of food and necessities—gone!

40

THE RUSH TO LEAVE

The wind had calmed, but the sea was running high—roiling, ugly water with branches and whole trees smashing against the bank.

Captain Lane ordered a crew to row him out to Admiral Drake. He sat gray-faced in the small boat as the rowers pulled hard and Andrew, Tremayne, and Mr. Harriot waded alongside, pushing it off against the pounding waves. Once the boat was launched, they pitched themselves in, soaked like a pack of wet dogs. The captain didn't look much better. He wore no finery.

The *Elizabeth Bonaventure*'s deck looked like the *Tyger*'s after her grounding. Teams of sailors chopped and slashed away wreckage of masts, spars, jibs, booms, and tackle as others hurried lumber and fittings to the sweating carpenters. Coils of rope and mounds of canvas lay by the hatches.

"We have nothing to sail with," the admiral muttered. "We're stuck here like a molting grub until these men grow us our new wings. The hull is sound, though, and the pumps are working. With luck she'll be rigged and ready before the next storm hits," he said, looking up.

The morning's blue sky had turned dull pewter.

"But for the skill of my sea captains, we'd all have wrecked onshore," said Sir Francis. "As it was, we took more cuts, bruises, and broken bones than we got storming St. Augustine!"

"We lost the *Francis,*" the captain said, pointing. "I'll have those people hanged for mutiny!"

The admiral shook his head.

"Given that storm, no jury in England will convict. It was the sea captain's order. He'll say he left these waters to save his ship."

As Captain Lane went *"Pfft,"* Sir Francis looked up sharply. "I would not vote to convict them, sir!"

Andrew and Tremayne exchanged glances as the captain stiffened, his face darkening. Before he could say anything, the admiral pointed at the sky. "More weather threatens, Captain. We must be off too!

"I can leave you supplies and another vessel. She's bigger, though. Not so handy for exploring. Or I can return you all to England.

"Answer within the hour! We depart in two," he yelled as he hurried forward to direct the stepping of a new mast.

The sky was low and ugly again. "A sign from an angry God," one of the rowers muttered as they worked their way back to shore. Andrew watched to see what the captain would do. Ordinarily, Captain Lane would have slapped the man or given worse for that. As it was, he sat unseeing, hearing nothing.

Once onshore he called an assembly. Everyone knew about the *Francis*'s escape.

"Admiral Drake offers more supplies and a larger vessel—though not so good for exploring," he announced. "We may take them and stay, or he'll carry us all back to England. Do we leave or stay?"

"Leave!" was the shout. There was not one voice for staying, not even Andrew's. He looked at Tremayne, then looked away.

Captain Lane signaled the admiral's flagship.

"Sound trumpets and ring the bell to call in all," he ordered. "We leave within the hour."

Soon the fleet's small boats could be seen dropping into water like eggshells to collect the explorers. All was uproar and disorder as men scurried to gather the few things they could save.

Sky stood watching as Andrew helped Tremayne

and Mr. Harriot stuff a trunk willy-nilly with papers, specimens, dried plants, the journal of the year's exploring, and a string of pearls for the Queen.

"Will you go with us?" Andrew asked his friend. Sky nodded slowly.

"He goes with us," Andrew said, pointing to Sky.

Mr. Harriot shook his head. "No!"

"He can't stay," Andrew cried. "To the Indians he is no longer an Indian. They will not trust him. He can't go back to his village any more than Manteo can."

Tremayne and Mr. Harriot stared, silent.

"If he stays, I stay," Andrew said, sitting down.

Mr. Harriot put up his hands. "If you can get him aboard, so be it," he said. "I can do nothing for you."

Manteo helped the boys drag the trunk to the beach. Already a fleet of small boats was heading out with explorers.

Andrew was afraid Captain Lane would try to keep Sky back when it came time to muster. To his surprise, there was no muster.

He shoved Salt into his saddlebag. The dog was heavy and protesting. In with him went flute, music, and the drug root he'd dug with Sky the day before. He wrapped a clay pipe in his cap for America and hurried with Sky to join Mr. Harriot and Tremayne as they loaded the trunk and climbed into one of the last boats.

The wind had turned. As they pushed off, the sea fought them with drenching waves and whitecaps.

The sailors were scared. "That last storm nearly did for us, and here's another!"

Their boat rode low. Waves lapped in as it pitched and rolled, taking on more water than they could bail.

"Throw off your trunk!" the chief rower called. "Heave it or we'll swamp."

No one moved. The sailor closest to Andrew raised his oar. "It goes or you do!" he bellowed.

The boat lurched wildly as Andrew and Sky hove the trunk.

As they boarded the flagship, they heard the whisper: "We left three behind—the scouts and hunters on the mainland."

Andrew turned to Mr. Harriot. "How can we leave our people?"

"You heard Admiral Drake," he said. "He told the captain he would not take another storm here. He gave us a choice: stay or go. There wasn't time to fetch the others. It was leave them or we all got left."

That's why there was no muster. There was no need to count.

41

A BRIEF AND TRUE REPORT

They fed well on board—fresh bread, eggs, roast goat, apples, pork pies, suet pudding. Sir Francis saw to it they got fresh clothes—Spanish things from his raid on St. Augustine. The pioneers barbered each other and grew cheerfuller as they checked the admiral's chart marking their progress home.

Forty-one days after they'd lifted anchor off Roanoke Island, the *Elizabeth Bonaventure* hove into Plymouth harbor. She was expected. Since the *Francis*'s arrival days before, messengers had ridden day and night to get word to London. All of Plymouth was alert for Drake's return with his shipload of explorers. Word got to Stillwell Farm. Andrew's parents hurried to the port, collecting Rebecca on the way.

People milled around in a great hubbub of yelling,

bells, drums, and trumpets as the Roanoke men disembarked. They found their legs as wobbly on land as they'd been their first days on shipboard. Even Salt staggered.

They were darker and rougher-looking than the eager-faced men who'd embarked a year before. Their Spanish fashions made them look strange, but given what people at home had heard from the *Francis*'s folks, they were prepared for anything.

Sky was staring, wide-eyed and trembling, when Andrew took his hand. "We stay together!" Andrew said. Sky nodded and tried to smile.

"A horse!" Andrew yelled, pointing.

"So big!" Sky murmured.

With Sky in tow, Andrew found his people. He knew they'd be there. He tried to speak. His heart was full; no words would come. Rebecca was rounder and even more beautiful than he'd remembered her.

"This is my . . . This is Sky—the friend I wrote you about," he stammered.

Sky said nothing. For a moment they were all awkward together; then Andrew's mother laughed and threw her arms around the two of them.

"Your ear . . . ," she started to say. She caught herself. "You're broader and lankier!" she went on, stepping back to look at Andrew.

"All that food," Andrew said, smiling through tears. He snuffed and wiped his face as his mother handed him the cloth she'd just been using.

"We can't stay long," he added. He'd noticed Quinch, the messenger from Sir Walter, beckoning as he huddled with Mr. Harriot. "Sir Walter orders us to London."

"What about your trunks?" his father asked.

Andrew pointed to his saddlebag. "I travel light," he said, trying to laugh. They listened with open mouths and many exclamations as he gave a quick account of his last weeks in Virginia.

Mr. Harriot motioned him to where he stood with Tremayne.

"We'll be back as soon as we report to Sir Walter," Andrew said as he hurried off with Sky.

"I've got gossip from Quinch," Mr. Harriot said with a sour smile. "Our friends have worn out a dozen horses racing to London with news that there is no mine of gold, few pearls, no way through to the Orient, and the Indians do not love us for all we gave them goods and true religion.

"Worse, we are rumored to have behaved like Spaniards."

"Sir Walter has heard all this?" Andrew asked.

"That and more," Mr. Harriot replied.

"And the Queen?"

Mr. Harriot barked a dry laugh. "I venture she got news of us before Sir Walter did."

A man came up with three horses.

"We're off," said Mr. Harriot. "Manteo and Sky will come up later with the others."

"No," said Andrew. "Sky comes with me. We'll ride together," he said firmly as the Indian boy stared, bewildered, first at Andrew, then at Mr. Harriot.

The way Andrew spoke decided things. He helped Sky squeeze into the saddle with him.

For three days they rode hard from dawn to dark, chafed and sore, changing the winded horses every twenty miles, most of the time silent. Sky looked around like one in shock. Andrew thought about all that had happened and imagined their reception at Durham House.

He saw England through new eyes as they rode. He'd never thought before how green and settled it was, every field, hedgerow, road, and village showing the touch of generations. As they passed a school, they heard the children reciting in singsong together. Virginia was richer in its way and more full of promise for the likes of him, but it was silent and empty in its newness.

A giddy feeling of being a stranger in a familiar place came over him like a wave of cold seawater. Suddenly, without thinking, he reached inside his shirt and touched the bear claw tied around his neck. Then he smiled and patted Sky. His friend turned a little and nodded, keeping his grip tight.

In Virginia there was nothing like Stillwell Farm. Everything was provisional there, quickly built and just as quickly abandoned—the Indians' villages, lodges, even their fields. Andrew had felt himself a stranger in America, but now he knew: he belonged there. He could build Stillwell in Virginia two times over, three, more—with Sky's help and oxen and plows and pioneers. They'd bring music and new voices to the land. As they broke the soil, they'd break the silence.

It was dark when they arrived at Durham House. William was there to greet them, cheering and waving as they dismounted. James was all smiles as he ordered torches and men to take their mounts. He lifted Sky down and propped him while the Indian tried to regain his legs. Then James and Salt led them up to Sir Walter's turret.

"My Americans returned!" Sir Walter exclaimed as they came in.

"And Sky," said Andrew, pushing the shivering boy forward.

"Welcome, Sky!" boomed Sir Walter.

The Indian stared and said nothing as Andrew led him to a bench.

Pena's face worked as they laughed and hugged. Sir Walter took the dog in his lap as if they were old friends.

"Never mind what you lost," Sir Walter said when Mr. Harriot told him about the trunk. "Tell me what you found!"

He ordered suppers carried up and a mutton bone for Salt. Sky ate, fought sleep, then nodded off. The rest talked all night.

"Is the soil good?" Sir Walter asked. "Is Virginia vast and rich with new things beyond reckoning?"

"Yes," the travelers answered to every question. "Yes!"

"And you, Andrew," he said with a wink, "did you find landlords and sheriffs there?"

"No!" the boy exclaimed with a laugh.

The more they talked, the faster Sir Walter paced, his hands in fists pumping like a man preparing to fight.

"In their greedy ignorance, my explorers and enemies alike slander Virginia," he exclaimed. "We must teach those mockers that the richest land is that which feeds the most!

"Listen!" he said, spreading his arms wide. "The Spaniards haul in gold by the pound and silver by the ton—and what's happened? Their poor go hungry. Why? Because on the flood of treasure, prices rise like moored ships at high tide. Their farmers don't grow more food; they grow less and charge more for it, so the lesser people suffer. Pah!" he spat.

"Tell me again how fast their corn grows with little effort. And again about their tobacco, Mr. Harriot. And their medicines! You've tasted it, I hear.

"And the capture of Pemisapan? Tell me about that! And what became of Wanchese? Tell! Tell all!"

They told of their adventures and Wanchese's betrayal.

"And when he figured we were as good as dead," said Mr. Harriot, "starved and frozen on the river, he ran away. We passed him on our way down. After that we never saw him again."

Mr. Harriot pointed to Tremayne. "He will tell you about Pemisapan's end. He was with the captain's servant when that man caught the chief and took his head, Irish style."

As Tremayne finished his telling, he reached into

his coat. "So we bring you the chief's breastplate, sir," he said as he hung it around Sir Walter's neck. "You now wear wassador!"

For a moment Sir Walter was without words. He quickly took the thing off and jiggled it in his hands like it was hot. He did not put it back on. "A sad token," he murmured. "A reminder to do better."

Andrew opened the saddlebag he'd packed at Roanoke. He felt for the cap Pena had given him, then he smiled as he pulled it out and unwrapped something.

"I brought you their pipe to drink tobacco, sir."

"Ha!" exclaimed Sir Walter, smiling as he took it.

"And here is a pouch of last fall's crop," said Mr. Harriot. "Shall we smoke it?"

Sir Walter shook his head in wonder. "You three are Magi, truly!"

The men passed the pipe around. The room filled with blue smoke. The fumes inspired them.

"We'll go back!" Sir Walter exclaimed. "Next time on the Chesapeake, to a good harbor with folks who know what rich soil counts for and how to use it.

"But first we must clear away the weeds of rumor. Bad luck did us damage: the loss of the *Tyger*'s cargo, the supply delayed—but for those, it would have gone better with the Indians."

He opened his arms wide. "I ask you: do you believe Virginia's promise?"

Each swore he did.

"Then tell it!" Sir Walter roared so loud the dog jumped and Sky woke up, bewildered, gaping and staring about as he tried to remember where he was.

"Gallant words printed will crush a thousand rumors!" Sir Walter thundered. "Be quick! Write what you've told me tonight. Write Virginia's promise so vivid as to set minds afire! Empty your trunks of memory on the page. Show Virginia in her glory—her vastness, her trees, meadows, fish, game. And her people. Show them not as savages but as our friends—as they will be if we are not necessitous!"

"Go now!" Sir Walter ordered.

He rang his bell.

"James! Get them fed, then take this one to Mistress Witkens," he said, putting his arm around Sky. "I can't have my newest page going around looking like a Spaniard," he laughed.

"I'll take him," Andrew said. To Sky he whispered, "I'll stay with you. Don't be afraid."

When the four travelers finally left the turret, there were layers of yellow, rose, and peach along the line of sunrise.

The following days went by in a blur as they wrote

to redeem Virginia. It was like writing the appeal to the Queen, only now there was no imagining. Instead of gold and dreams, they told what they had found—deep soil and broad rivers, iron and tobacco, medicines, fish in plenty, crabs, oysters, sturgeon seven feet long, sunflowers a foot across, nuts, berries, corn, potatoes, peanuts, silk grass, groves of giant oak to build ships with, stands of pine for masts. They wrote about the tree that blooms tulips and the vast clumps of blueberries and strawberries they'd found. And the Indians: Mr. Harriot told their ways and their religion.

They dedicated their "Brief and True Report" to

"the Adventurers, Favorers, and Well-Wishers of the enterprise for the inhabiting and planting in Virginia." They filled it with their sharpest rememberings. They made nothing up.

"Take Sky and go home for a week," Sir Walter told Andrew when they delivered the book. "When you return, you'll be my secretary."

"And Sky?" Andrew asked.

"He and Pena are great friends already. He'll teach Pena how the Indians grow their foods."

The report spread the truth about Virginia. Within months it was being read all over Europe. When Sir Walter announced his offer of five hundred acres to every settler, planters came forward with their families. Investors came forward too—foreigners, merchants, and courtiers, even the Queen herself, some said—but as before, Sir Walter would have to pay the most to get things started.

"Virginia empties my pockets," he mused one chilly morning as he worked with Andrew in the turret, ordering provisions for the expedition to settle. "But I will live to see England in America, lad, and you'll be part of it!"

"Yes," said Andrew, breathing deep. "Yes!"

God speed you well and send you fair weather
And that again we may meet together.

—Thomas Harriot,
the ending of "The Three Sea Marriages," 1595(?)

AUTHOR'S NOTE

Raleigh's Page is a fiction. Walter Raleigh (*Ralegh* is how it was spelled in his time) had pages, and Thomas Harriot had a secretary, but Andrew is an invention, as are Tremayne, Pena, and Sky. The larger historical events are roughly accurate (except I have Doctor Dee fleeing to Bohemia a year after he actually left). The major figures are pretty much as documents of the time presented them.

The 1585 expedition was sent to explore and gather facts about Virginia, not to settle. The push to settle came much later, although a first group of families went out in 1587. Preparations to fight the Spanish Armada in 1588 disrupted the crucial resupply shipments, and the colony failed. No survivor was ever found. Not until 1607 did the reconstituted Virginia Company attempt another colony, that time at Jamestown.

A note on sources: the best are what the participants themselves wrote about their experiences. For
Andrew's story we have three. The first is Raleigh's appeal to the Queen for permission to go, which he composed with Richard Hakluyt: *A Discourse on Western
Planting.* It was written as a state paper for the Queen
and seen by few others. It remained pretty much un-
known until it was found in Boston in 1877. An excellent modern edition is *Discourse of Western Planting,*
edited by David B. and Alison M. Quinn (London:
Hakluyt Society, 1993), which includes photographs of
the original so you can see the copyists' work.

The next important contemporary source is
Captain Ralph Lane's letter to Sir Walter describing
the expedition: "Account of the particularities of the
imployments of the English men left in Virginia by
Richard Grenvill under the charge of Master Ralph
Lane Generall of the same, from the 17 of August
1585, until the 18 of June 1586, at which time they de-
parted the Countrey; sent and directed to Sir Walter
Ralegh." Lane's letter can be found in *The First
Colonists,* edited by A. L. Rowse (London: Folio Society, 1986).

Then there's Thomas Harriot's advertisement for
Virginia, which I have his imagined secretary, Andrew,

help him compose: *A Briefe and True Report of the new found land of Virginia* (London, 1588). *The First Colonists* has this too.

Richard Hakluyt, principal author of *A Discourse on Western Planting,* also compiled a collection of exploration narratives that gives vivid pictures of the English explorers' hopes and difficulties: *The Principal Navigations, Voyages, Traffics, and Discoveries of the English Nation, Made by Sea or over Land to the Remote and farthest Distant Quarters of the Earth at Any Time within the Compass of These 1500 Years* (London, 1589). A good selection is *The Portable Hakluyt's Voyages,* edited by Irwin R. Blacker (New York: Viking Press, 1965).

What about contemporary images? A painter named John White accompanied the 1585 expedition and made a number of pictures. Although many were lost in the frenzy to leave that saw Mr. Harriot's trunk dumped overboard, some survived. While a few are reproduced in *The First Colonists,* the best source is *America, 1585: The Complete Drawings of John White,* compiled by Paul Hulton (London: British Museum Publications, 1984).

You'll find excellent, compact biographical sketches of the principal participants in the English

Oxford Dictionary of National Biography, or the *DNB* (Oxford: Oxford University Press, 2004)—some of the best history writing I know.

For general background, see J. H. Elliott, *Empires of the Atlantic World: Britain and Spain in America, 1492–1830* (New Haven: Yale University Press, 2006). In addition, I relied on the *DNB;* A. L. Rowse, *The Elizabethans and America* (London: Macmillan, 1959); *Life in Shakespeare's England,* edited by John Dover Wilson (Cambridge: University Press, 1911); Liza Picard, *Elizabeth's London: Everyday Life in Elizabethan London* (London: Weidenfield & Nicholson, 2003); and Giles Milton, *Big Chief Elizabeth: How England's Adventurers Gambled and Won the New World* (London: Hodder and Stoughton, 2000).

For information about the Indians, I used Thomas Harriot's *Briefe and True Report;* John Lawson, *The History of Carolina* (London: 1706); Mark Catesby, "Of the Aborigines of America," in his *Natural History of Carolina* (London: 1771, Vol. I); Helen C. Rountree, *The Powhatan Indians of Virginia* (Norman: University of Oklahoma Press, 1989); Karen Ordahl Kupperman, *Indians and English* (Ithaca, N.Y.: Cornell University Press, 2000); and Roger Owen, James J. F. Deetz, and Anthony D. Fisher, *The North American Indians* (New York: Macmillan, 1967).

For Sir Walter Raleigh: the *DNB;* [John] *Aubrey's Brief Lives,* edited by Oliver Lawson Dick (Ann Arbor: University of Michigan Press, 1957); J. H. Adamson and H. F. Folland, *The Shepherd of the Ocean* (Boston: Gambit, 1969); Martin A. Hume, *Sir Walter Raleigh: The British Dominion of the West* (New York: Alfred A. Knopf, 1926); Margaret Irwin, *That Great Lucifer* (New York: Harcourt, Brace, and Company, 1960); David B. Quinn, *Raleigh and the British Empire* (London: Hodder and Stoughton, 1947); and George Garrett, *Death of the Fox* (New York: Doubleday, 1971)—an inspired book.

For Queen Elizabeth: J. E. Neale, *Queen Elizabeth* (New York: Harcourt, Brace, and Company, 1934), and her own *The Sayings of Queen Elizabeth,* edited by Frederick Chamberlin (London: The Bodley Head, 1923). Quotations attributed to the Queen are hers; the context is mine.

For Thomas Harriot: the *DNB* and Muriel Rukeyser, *The Traces of Thomas Harriot* (New York: Random House, 1971).

For Doctor Dee, I relied on the *DNB.* He is one of the most interesting and appealing figures of his time (1527–1608), half medieval, half modern in outlook—half magician, half scientist as he attempted to make gold from lesser metals, experimented with numbers, codes, and chemicals, and spoke with his "angels" and lesser spirits through a globe of smoky crystal and a black mirror of coal he kept in a leather case (it can be seen at the British Museum). Queen Elizabeth consulted him about her toothaches and had him perform an astrological calculation to select her coronation day. She came more than once to his home at Mortlake to learn some of his secrets. He was suspected of treason and heresy, and many in his time took him to be a conjuror—an agent of the devil—a reputation he got early on when he arranged a trick that sent an actor flying up from the stage (probably on ropes the audience couldn't see). "They call me a companion of the hellhounds, and a caller, and a conjuror of wicked and damned spirits," he lamented late in life, protesting that all his marvelous feats were naturally contrived. His lectures were so popular, folks crowded outside at the windows to hear. He charmed Andrew; he charms me.

Specific notes:

Chapter 1, the scholar Richard Eden (1521?–1576): I have Andrew's teacher, Tremayne, telling his students about Eden; translations of Spanish accounts of the New World were published in 1577 as *The History of*

Travel in the East and West Indies. Eden was one of the early instigators of English colonization.

Chapter 3, enclosure men: for a good description, I went to James Shapiro's *1599: A Year in the Life of William Shakespeare* (London: Faber and Faber, 2005), 271–73. "Shakespeare's 'As You Like It' made clear to contemporary audiences the plight of enclosure men. Elizabethans knew what it meant when old Adam staggered onstage at the beginning of Act II, scene vi, exhausted and starving in the Forest of Arden, and told Orlando, 'I can go no further. Oh, I die for food! Here lie I down and measure out my grave'. . . . The early acts of the play circle back time and again to the problems caused by vagrancy and hunger, including Orlando's angry words when Adam first suggests that they turn itinerant: 'What, wouldst thou have me go and beg my food? Or with a base and boist'rous sword enforce a thievish living on the common road? This I must do or know not what to do.'"

Chapter 4, Durham House: From *Aubrey's Brief Lives:* "Durham House was a noble palace; after he [Raleigh] came to his greatness he lived there or in some apartment of it. I well remember his study, which was a little turret that looked into and over the Thames, and had the prospect which is pleasant perhaps as any in the World, and which not only refreshes the eie-sight but cheeres the spirits, and (to speake my mind) I beleeve enlarges an ingeniose man's thoughts" (op. cit., 254).

Concerning Raleigh's interest in medicine, Aubrey again: "Sir Walter Raleigh was a great Chymist, and amongst some MSS. receipts I have seen some secrets from him. He studyed most in his Sea-Voyages, where he carried always a Trunke of Bookes along with him, and had nothing to divert him. He made an excellent Cordiall, good in Feavers, etc. Mr. Robert Boyle haz the recipe, and makes it and does great Cures by it. . . . He was no Slug; without doubt he had a wonderful waking spirit, and a great judgement to guide it" (ibid).

The book of Spanish medicinal plants Raleigh had Andrew digest was fully titled, in its first English translation, *Joyfull Newes out of the Newe-Found Worlde*. It was compiled in Seville by a distinguished Spanish physician named Nicholas Monardes (1493– 1588). For years, travelers returning from what we now call Central and South America brought Monardes bark, roots, seeds, flowers, leaves, and whole plants together with reports of their curative powers. His *Joyfull Newes* promised "present remedie for all diseases. . . ." His chief remedy was tobacco, and his essay on it makes curious reading today. Raleigh's copy was a translation made by John Frampton and published in 1577.

Chapter 25: The Star Singers figure in Dutch engravings of that period. Their chant is a poem by Ian Hamilton Finlay.

Chapter 30: The medicine root was probably ginseng. See Alan W. Armstrong, ed., *"Forget Not Mee & My Garden . . .": Selected Letters, 1725–1768, of Peter Collinson, F.R.S.* (Philadelphia: American Philosophical Society, 2002), 70.

Chapter 31: Captain Lane's "wassador" was unrefined copper. Most was dark red but some was pale, almost yellow. It was prized for jewelry and gifts to the Indian gods.

Chapter 32: The grass they peeled strands of silk from was probably what we know as yucca.

Chapter 33: The priests may have put dried jimsonweed blossoms on Mr. Harriot and added its seeds and leaves to the fire. The smoke would have been mildly hallucinogenic.

When Captain Lane led the late-winter expedition in search of wassador, he would have followed a course roughly like that shown on the map on page 327. They would have rowed north up Roanoke Sound, aiming west when they came to the much larger Albemarle Sound, paddling about forty miles—nearly its entire length—against stiff, late-winter winds and stinging snow before they turned north into the Chowan River, leading up to Chief Menatonon's head-quarters.

VIRGINIA

← – – – – – –

ROUTE OF CAPTAIN LANE'S
1586 LATE WINTER EXPEDITION
TO CHIEF MENATONON IN
SEARCH OF WASSADOR.

ROANOKE ISLAND

Special thanks to Frances S. Pollard, director of library services, Virginia Historical Society; to Karin Wulf, book review editor of *William and Mary Quarterly* and associate professor of history and American Studies at the College of William and Mary; and to the librarians at the Neilson Library, Smith College, Northampton, Massachusetts. Thanks also to Kristen Depken, to copy editor Jenny Golub, and to Joe Rayo at the Hayden Planetarium for celestial advice. Martha Armstrong, A. L. Hart, and Kate Klimo brought Andrew to life.